I0546170

Hard as Stone
Dwarven Erotica

EDITED BY
JULIE COX

CIRCLET PRESS, INC.
CAMBRIDGE, MA

Contents

Introduction

by Julie Cox

ANYONE WHO HAS PERUSED a fanfiction site will quickly learn this fundamental truth: the most unexpected things can be sexy.

Elves? Definitely sexy. Shapeshifters? Easily sexy. Vampires? Have their moments still. Aliens? Um, they have potential. Satyrs? HA, of course they are. Dwarves? Hrm. Until recently, I would have said no. Then I wrote "Wizard's Staff" and surprised myself. Yes, dwarves can definitely be sexy.

And the Tolkien corner of the fanfiction universe seemed to agree with me. After all, dwarves were stalwart, strong, and mysterious. They had just enough cultural detail to give writers a place to start, a spark, without being so specific that it limited story potential. Nearly human, with a twist.

I was delighted by the responses to the call for submissions for the dwarf anthology. In particular, it was wonderful to see the variety—lesbian stories, gay stories, stories that defied both biological sex and sociological gender. Touching love stories, brief encounters, harrowing danger, humor, *magic*. Some came to me rough, like uncut diamonds, some just needed a polish, and one special gem needed absolutely no changes at all. (Hint: it wasn't mine.)

"Stolen Days" does indeed feel like a stolen moment, a delightful story full of affection and pleasure and devotion, told in a comfortable tone that makes one feel like curling up beside a hearth.

"Rainbows in Hollywood" combines a nearly modern setting with fantasy magic in a truly unique and beautiful fashion. It is like an unexpected glimpse of magic in the real world, startling yet somehow familiar.

"Ash and Elm" reminds us that dwarves are, after all, fairy tale creatures. Its lyrical style is as beautiful and delicate as its setting; it blends natural magic and otherworldly eroticism seamlessly. It feels like an old story, one we should already know. I see shades of Neil Gaiman and Lord Dunsany in this one.

"Wizard's Staff" takes a look at dwarven sex magic, with runes and obscenity and, uh, a staff. Our clever heroes make do with what they have to get the job done. One night stands can be hot, but longtime lovers know how to push each other's buttons. (Also it's mine, so obviously I think highly of it.)

"Cave Dwellers" takes human ideas of gender and biological sex and says "to hell with that." It is a unique, fun take on why we so rarely see dwarf women. OR DO WE? Told in a bawdy, brash tone, it was one of my favorites from the first time I read it.

"To Those Who Move Mountains" has interesting things to say about dwarven technology and culture, against a background of danger and promise. Even more interesting to us, of course, is how those things bring lovers together in times of distress.

Every collection of stories needs a darker story in its ranks, and ours is "Don't Screw the Messenger." Lots of different fairy tale threads cross each other in this story—evil queens, houses full of dwarves, spinning gold, the power of names, transformation, and betrayal.

"Of Greed and Eager Things" closes our collection with yet another unexpected turn of dwarven sexuality in a fantasy setting familiar yet unique, with dwarven royalty, danger, and adventure. Destiny awaits.

I hope you enjoy these stories, and I hope you discover something sexy that you might not have considered sexy before.

Stolen Days

by TS Porter

EILIR SMILED AS HER dusty boots finally carried her around the corner of the weedy overgrown path and she saw the squat stone cottage nestled like a toadstool beneath the gnarled branches of an ancient walnut tree. A thin trail of smoke issued from a chimney, wreathing it in a bluish haze and the scent of coal in the still summer air.

She could hear rhythmic clanging and sidled up to the building's attached blacksmithing workshop as quietly as she could—and that was *very* quiet. She climbed silently up to sit in the wide stone windowsill, unnoticed, and watched.

To watch Tellou work was a vice she so rarely had the chance to indulge.

The smith's solid form was lit red with the coals of the forge and the glowing heat of the metal she worked. Her face looked stern, her concentration fully absorbed by her craft. Tellou's dark hair and beard, touched with the first frost of silver, hung in a few simple braids, half-unraveled in the heat of the forges. Eilir's fingers *itched* to braid them up properly... or undo them completely. A small bead of sweat rolled down the side of Tellou's neck to soak into the heavily scorched leather apron that covered the broad curves of her chest, belly, and hips.

The light of the fire gleamed off the powerful corded muscles of her bare forearms and biceps. The smith's hammer fell again and again in perfectly measured blows as she folded the steel she worked.

Tellou reached into the forge without looking, her thick fingers digging through the glowing coals to draw out a cherry-red steel bar. She idly knocked the coals off it before she incorporated it into the piece she was working. Eilir bit her lips to prevent herself from gasping and giving herself away. She knew that Tellou came from a long line of Dwarves who bore the Fire's Blessing, that the heat of smithing could not harm her, but it still made her stomach clench and her skin prickle every time she watched it.

Eilir waited, watching the finest and most secretive smith in the realm at her work, until Tellou seemed to decide the folded steel had been worked enough for one day and set it aside to cool. Tellou dropped her brawny shoulders into a pose of relaxation and rolled her neck, settling with her head thrown back and her face toward the ceiling. She groaned as the tension of her work left her.

"Mastress Argantel." Eilir's voice was the carefully clipped accent of Ramaria city as she used Tellou's proper name and title, her tone just this side of a sneer. She did not even flutter an eyelash as the smith whirled on her with a snarl, hammer raised as if to throw. Eilir sniffed dismissively at the simplicity of the forge she found herself in.

"My knives require sharpening. You do have the proper supplies in this... hovel?" she asked, as though she expected the smith wouldn't have the tools and skill to make *nails*.

Tellou lowered her hammer, her jaw tensing beneath her beard and her dark eyes burning as she took two menacing steps forward.

"I do," she said roughly, "but you'll be paying a pretty penny to be worth *my* time, City Girl."

"Well!" Eilir said haughtily. "The likes of you should be happy for my business—but if the promise of my recommendation isn't enough for you perhaps we could come to *another arrangement*..." She let her voice drop huskily at the end, watching the smith from under her lashes as she trailed her fingertips meaningfully up the inside of her thigh.

Tellou broke first—she always did. She snorted as she bit her lips, then gave up and threw her head back to laugh that deep belly laugh that never failed to warm Eilir clean through. She dropped her hammer on the nearest work surface and reached for her.

"How can you *say* those things?" she laughed, and Eilir pulled her in with a smile. Tellou's skin was still scorching hot from the forges, and Eilir whimpered as big burning hands ran down the back of her body. She wrapped her legs around the smith's waist, the core of her strength. The heat of her was nearly painful through Eilir's thin travel clothes and she pulled Tellou in close, branding the feel of her into her skin as she lifted her face for a kiss.

"I *missed* you," she whispered as Tellou's lips met hers, dropping her Ramaria accent and manner so she was just herself, born to nothing here in the tiny village of Meadowsweet.

Tellou's mouth tasted of metal and smoke and Eilir moaned into the heat of it. Her arms found their home around the smith's shoulders, petting those beloved messy braids.

"Eilir," Tellou whispered, her warm brown eyes soft as she cradled her face in her rough hands, peppering kisses across her forehead and cheeks. "Eilir... my little Llio." The name was achingly soft on her lips.

Llio.

Yes.

Here she did not have to be Eilir, the stinging butterfly. Here she did not navigate the battering winds of truths and lies, seeing everything, with the brightness of her wings disguising the deadly sharpness of her knives.

Here she was simple, beloved, *Llio.* Tellou's calloused hands lifted the weight of Eilir from her.

"My Tellou," she whispered Argantel's pet name back to her, a name *no one* else was allowed to call her. A better name. A soft name for a lover and not the steel-sharp name of a smith forever driven to perfect the imperfectible.

Llio could hold Argantel and let her be *Tellou*, and Tellou could hold Eilir and let her be *Llio*.

Just for a little while.

Tellou nuzzled noses with her and fondly tugged on one of Llio's beard braids. "I wasn't expecting you back so soon," she said.

Llio angled her mouth up for another kiss, a soft one with her legs still wrapped tight around Tellou's solid waist, nothing but gentle lips as she let her love hold her safe. "Something came up unexpectedly," she whispered. "I had to tell the Crown, she gave me a few days."

"Nothing dangerous, I hope? The Kingdoms *are* at peace," Tellou said hopefully, and Llio just smiled at her. For all Tellou was older, living so deeply immersed in her work had left her beautifully innocent.

"You know I can't tell you anything," Llio murmured, and she wouldn't have even if she could. Tellou never needed to know of working partners dying to get information to her, of betrayal and constant distrust, of running for her life when things went wrong and thanking every day she didn't add to the trail of bodies behind her. She would never put the weight of that on gentle Tellou.

...but these were *Eilir* thoughts, and Llio pushed them away.

The smith rolled her eyes at the old argument they didn't actually get into anymore, and picked Llio up to carry her out of the forge. Llio squeaked, she always did, and Tellou chucked. Llio was no bird-light Fae, but Tellou carried her as easily as though she were one instead of a solid Dwarf with iron in her very bones.

Llio nuzzled her face into Tellou's neck beneath her messy braids, ran a hand down her lover's burly arm, and enjoyed her strength. Only here with Tellou could Llio relax, let go, and let *someone else* be the strong one.

There was a rain barrel for washing up out behind the little cottage. Llio had gotten Tellou's soot all over her, in addition to the dust of the road. The water in the barrel was dark brown from fallen walnut leaves Tellou hadn't bothered to fish out, but it still smelled fresh enough.

Llio refused to get down when Tellou let her go, clinging tight to her to beg just one more kiss. Tellou was laughing as she gave it to her, nuzzling noses again with her warm eyes shining.

Llio dropped to the ground to stand on her own, getting an affectionate squeeze to her middle. Tellou removed her scorched leather apron, hanging it on the nearby peg Llio had hung there for just that purpose so long ago. The smith kicked her boots off and shrugged out of her simple linen dress, standing naked in the filtered sunlight and utterly unselfconscious of that fact. Tellou never had been able to see herself, not the way Llio saw her. Her body, to her, was just a convenient tool for her smith work. She took care of it, as she did all her tools, but sometimes she needed reminding that it was flesh and not a machine of iron and will.

She would allow Llio to do that.

Tellou poured a bucket of water over herself, scrubbing the forge soot from the warm coppery sandstone of her skin. Shining beads of water clung to the thick sculptured muscles of her arms and shoulders, the softness of her heavy breasts, the round strength of her belly and the generous curves of her hips. Llio ached to reach out and touch, to reacquaint herself, but she controlled herself.

They both knew the steps of this dance.

When she was satisfied with her cleanliness Tellou shook the water from herself and turned to Llio. "Now you," she said, cradling the sides of Llio's face with her damp hands.

Llio nodded. "I trust you," she answered, and was rewarded with the warm brush of lips against her own for it. It was so *so* hard, in a world where she could trust no one, but this was Tellou. She'd loved her since she was an awkward, scuff-kneed adolescent sneaking away to watch the smith at her work. This was Tellou, who couldn't lie to save her own life. Tellou who lived for her work and cared about almost nothing else. Even if she had *wanted* to Tellou wouldn't know how to betray Llio.

Tellou began by unwinding the complex knot Llio kept her thousand tiny braids in. She carefully removed the decorative enameled combs that hid poison pins, setting them aside. Tellou took away the small stiletto that lived nestled against the nape of Llio's neck, thick fingers gentle against her scalp, and checked the condition of the blade before she set that aside too.

She unlaced Llio's bodice and took away the knives hidden within it. Tellou took the matched daggers she wore openly strapped to her thighs, her boots and the knives hidden there. Tellou took every last knife and piece of clothing Llio wore until Llio was as naked as she was, and Llio let her—the only person in the world she'd let disarm her while she lived and breathed. The only person who knew how many knives she carried and where, the person who'd made them to her exact needs and specifications.

"There's my little Llio, " Tellou said approvingly, her big hand stroking down Llio's shoulder—sandstone against hematite. Llio would probably never match the solid beauty of the smith, but she wasn't too bad. The softness in her love's eyes seemed to disagree, watching her with a worshipful concentration that never failed to make her blush. Tellou scooped up a bucket of water to wash the dust of the road from her, and Llio jumped and squeaked at the coldness of the water. She wasn't *used* to it anymore, the way Tellou was.

"Going soft on me, City Girl?" Tellou asked, laughter in her voice, and Llio poked at her ticklish sides in retaliation. Tellou growled warningly, but Llio didn't stop until Tellou was forced pin her against the heavy water barrel and kiss her. Tellou was big and strong and solid, warm against the coolness of Llio's damp skin, bare skin so soft against her own. Llio moaned as Tellou had her mouth. Nothing could match the perfection of her heat and passion in those rare moments when it was all focused on Llio. She wrapped her arms around Tellou, arching into the hands that stroked her back, cradled the back of her head. She'd missed this so much, missed Tellou and missed the luxury of letting her guard down. She could feel the quiet heat of her arousal, slowly growing ever since she set eyes on the smith, building warm in her belly and tight down her thighs.

"Let that be a warning to you," Tellou said when they finally parted, breathless herself. She tried to sound gruff, but her voice betrayed how close she was to laughing.

"I'll be good," Llio promised, looking up at Tellou coyly from under her lashes.

"Liar," Tellou accused softly, smiling, and Llio nodded solemnly in agreement. Tellou snorted a laugh, shaking her head as she stepped back.

"Let me finish," Tellou said, and Llio nodded again. She let Tellou wash her everywhere, the smith's fingers tracing her scars—counting them. Llio was not allowed to *tell* anything about her work, but there was no part of her body she would hide from Tellou. She let Tellou search her, though she did not have any new scars for her to find.

Not this time, close as it had been.

While Tellou's attention was taken with Llio's body, she began unbraiding Tellou's messy silver-frosted braids.

Tellou's hair was gorgeous, thick and heavy with a few more pale-gleaming strands to decorate it every year. Llio ran her fingers through it as she took the braids out, and Tellou made a happy little rumble at the attention.

As thorough as Tellou's exploration of Llio's body was, her touch was anything but clinical. Big hands rough from the forge cupped Llio's breasts, stroked gently down the curves of her body, giving a little squeeze here and there when they found something they particularly liked. Llio had goosebumps from more than just the coolness of the water by the time Tellou was done, and by the way Tellou looked at her she knew it too. Her smile as she straightened back up was as close as her sweet face could make to a leer.

She reached for Llio, but Llio was faster and combat trained—she twisted through the larger woman's grasp and knocked her back against the stone wall of the cottage.

"*My* turn," she said, and saw the familiar moment surprise on Tellou's face. Tellou was so used to not considering her own body it never failed to catch her off guard when Llio *did*. Left to her own devices she would have continued using it as a tool, a tool for Llio's pleasure because that's what had her attention at the moment, but still a tool. She would not have considered that it was for her own pleasure too.

It was Llio's duty and pleasure to remind her.

She started by nuzzling beneath Tellou's loose unbraided beard to kiss down the tender side of her neck as she filled her hands to overflowing with the softness of Tellou's breasts. She gave them a good squeeze before she moved on to stroke the rest of her body. She took her time, a feast like Tellou was meant to be savored. Llio slid one of her thighs between Tellou's powerful legs, just pressing herself as tightly as she could to the strength of Tellou's body.

Tellou shuddered, her moan holding that edge of surprise it always did after Llio had been away for a while. She was always sensitive, going untouched for so long, and Llio was not afraid to take advantage of that. She nibbled on Tellou's neck and moved with her, their bodies undulating together as the smith began to squirm. One of Llio's hands found its way back to Tellou's breast as she switched sides of her neck to give equal attention to both sides. She gently circled her thumb over one hard-pebbled dark nipple and smiled against Tellou's skin as her hips bucked in reaction, rubbing the heat of her sex against Llio's well-placed thigh.

"Llio!" Tellou gasped, following with an inarticulate groan. The fingers of one hand were buried in Llio's tumbling pale braids, the other was spread wide on Llio's back, holding her in tight and close. Llio repeated the touches had given her that reaction, flexing her thigh between Tellou's legs and soaking in the larger woman's reactions. Arms

that could have crushed Llio cradled her as Tellou whimpered at the
sensations she just *forgot* her body could give her. Tellou pressed into
every touch, every kiss and caress Llio gave her. When she was quiver-
ing all over, her head thrown back and the cottage wall the only thing
keeping her upright, her slickness painted thick where she rubbed on
Llio's thigh—Llio moved down Tellou's body.

The soft moss that grew up to the cottage wall was not uncomfortable to kneel on, which Llio appreciated.

Tellou keened, legs spreading wider, as she realized what was about
to happen. Her breath caught as Llio teased with a breath ghosting
against her warm-flushed sex. She breathed the beloved scent of her
lover, just once, admiring the sparkling dewdrops that caught in the
graying curls that framed her.

Llio licked softly, probing delicately between her lips to taste her.
Tellou was warm, silky smooth and wet with that smokey-metal flavor
that came from so many hours at the forge. Tellou's work was a part of
her, written throughout her, but Llio could steal her away for a little
while.

Llio held onto Tellou's thigh for leverage as she nosed higher,
searching with her tongue for the center of her lover's pleasure, her
gemstone. It was plump and warm, ready for her, and she was glad for
her grip on Tellou's thigh so she was not thrown off as the smith's hips
bucked. Already Tellou was reduced to deep gasping moans, her big
hands clenching and unclenching where she braced herself on the cottage wall, and Llio flicked her tongue in relentless circles.

Tellou's whole body shook, an earthquake in her bones, big muscles
clenching across her body in waves. She was beautiful, so beautiful from
between her legs as Llio held tight and rode her through the moans and
cries of her climax. Llio pushed Tellou as high as she was able, until her
lover could take no more and pushed her away with a whimper, hips
squirming away instead of pressing in.

Llio began to pull herself back up to her feet, but Tellou was sinking down at the same time and she found herself engulfed in her big arms, lying in the moss. Tellou whimpered wordlessly, still riding the aftershocks with little trembles traveling through her. She buried her face in Llio's mass of pale braids and held her close and tight.

"I forget," Tellou whispered, when she'd finally gathered herself enough to be able to form sentences again, laughing at herself a little. She kissed Llio deeply, humming at the flavor of herself on her lips. Tellou rested her forehead against Llio's, her warm eyes shining so close. "I always think 'she can't be that good,' and then you're *better*."

"Mm." Llio preened, stroking down Tellou's body as she wrapped a leg around hers to pull her just that little bit closer. There was a sweet ache in her lower belly, her own patient arousal begging for attention, hungry for touch.

In just a moment Tellou would....

They kissed again, gentle and warm, and *there* was the sudden spark in Tellou's eyes as she remembered. One big hand stroked down and squeezed Llio's bottom, thigh shifting between her legs.

"Oh, " Tellou breathed, her smile bordering on the predatory. "Oh my Llio, it's *your* turn."

She stood, carrying Llio with her into the house as though she weighed nothing, and utterly unconcerned with the green stains on their bodies from the moss as she tossed Llio on the big bed. Gorgeous solid Tellou took a moment to stand back and admire Llio as though *she* were the beautiful one between them before she turned to dig through a drawer.

"Where did, ah!" Tellou emerged with a smile and a delicately colored glass cock crafted by the finest glassblower in Ramaria city. Llio moaned at the sight of it, her legs parting as her muscles clenched. Llio could almost feel bad that she got so much more from the present she'd bought for Tellou, but Tellou didn't seem to mind. Tellou crawled over

Llio, pausing to rub her cheeks against both her breasts before she nestled the smooth glass cock between them.

"Warm this up," Tellou requested, and Llio nodded. She placed one hand over it to hold it in place while she reached for Tellou, angling her face for a kiss. She would never get tired of kissing in these rare times when she had all of the smith's attention. Tellou bracketed her, so big and strong with all the fire of her passion focused on Llio. One rough hand ran down Llio's body, stroking back up the inside of her thigh and big fingers finally coming to rest against the long-waiting slickness of her sex.

Llio moaned, a tremble traveling through her as she spread her legs wider, begging. Tellou chuckled, eyes hot and bright, and she *didn't* move her fingers. She wouldn't, not until she was ready, and Llio whimpered.

Tellou would study her as intensely as she studied her metalwork, take her apart and *know* her. She would mold the molten heat of her into whatever she wanted, and Llio would let her.

The only person in the world she would let her guard down for.

"I trust you," she breathed against Tellou's lips, not flinching from the fire in her lover's gorgeous dark eyes.

Llio straddled Tellou's belly. The smith was sprawled loose-limbed beneath her, eyes closed and a small smile on her lips. Llio gently stroked her fingers through the soft strands of Tellou's silver-touched beard, braiding it close along the bottom edges of her jaw and gathering it into a long bullwhip braid on her chin. Her beard grew in so evenly, its natural untended shape elegant enough to make the finest courtesans of Ramaria city weep for jealousy, and Tellou did nothing with it.

Tellou could have been one of them, if she'd wanted, a courtesan. *No one* could match her for strength and beauty. She could have bedded royalty and married into the finest circles—but that had never interested her. Tellou had taken herself away to the outskirts of little Meadowsweet where she could practice her smithwork undisturbed; until

Llio managed to insinuate herself in her life and steal away just a *piece* of her attention.

Tellou's eyes shot open, wide and unseeing. "But nickel could counteract the brittleness from the chromium!" she gasped, nearly dislodging Llio with her sudden attempt to sit up. Llio placed her hands on both sides of Tellou's face.

"Tellou... my Tellou," she crooned, and her love's brown eyes finally focused on Llio.

"My little Llio," Tellou answered, relaxing beneath her again as she reached up to wind a few of Llio's thousand tiny braids around a finger.

Tellou sighed and closed her eyes again, content to remain *Tellou* with Llio for a little longer and not run back to her forge to be Mastress Argantel, finest smith in the realm.

Llio smiled a little, a little sadly, as she resumed working on the bullwhip braid that was the height of fashion in Ramaria.

She could only hold Tellou for a *little* while—the quiet sorrow of all those Dwarves who loved those who lived in their work. They were the finest of craftspeople, but their attention was stolen away in moments. Soon the forge would call *Argantel* louder than Llio could call *Tellou,* and she would be forgotten as all the passionate intensity of that focus was shifted back where it had always belonged.

All Llio could do was learn to take comfort in the fact that she was the only one Tellou gave even this much to.

Llio could not complain, though. Tellou had to endure sending Llio away, again and again, and never knowing if this time was the time she didn't come home. Just a few stolen days and the Crown would call Eilir back.

She would be the stinging butterfly again, working to make sure there were no surprises; that the fragile peace between the Kingdoms did not fail. She would make sure the Fae were not attempting to revive the war dragons of legend, that the Goblins were not turning their particular genius toward machines of destruction, that none of the Dwarven nobles were planning on trespassing to mine for resources that were not theirs to take.

She would navigate the battering winds of truths and lies to be sure her Tellou and all those gentle Dwarves like her were safe.

...but these were *Eilir* thoughts, and Llio pushed them away.

Llio finished Tellou's braid and sat back to just look at her love. For a few days she would be simple, beloved, Llio—born to nothing here in the tiny village of Meadowsweet. She would wear her long braids loose, and simple linen dresses, and no knives, and make love with Tellou until both of them were too sore for even *one* more round. Llio would take care of her Tellou, cook for her, clean the walnut leaves out of the rain barrel, and maybe even weed the poor neglected garden if there was anything left under all the weeds.

For a few days she could have Tellou.

Llio smiled and gently stroked the side of the napping smith's face before shifting to lie on top of Tellou's strength and softness. She stroked a hand down the corded muscles of Tellou's arm, still hard even in relaxation. Llio smiled as she closed her eyes to rest too.

A few stolen days would be enough.

Rainbows in Hollywood

by Lacey M. Jeffers

GRANCIE CLOSED HER eyes, mouthed the words, and felt the magic coalesce around her. The world shifted. The smell of dead leaves and wet earth gave way to juniper, dust, and exhaust. Grancie could sense minerals close to the surface here and the dwarf in her urged her to investigate, but she resisted and found the road that led into the city. The stink of animal shit and rotting refuse was replaced by machine exhaust and although it burned her eyes, she preferred it.

She slipped the little book of magic back in her pocket.

When she had been in the world of Hollywood last time, Grancie saw a sign for hamburgers. She loved ham but had no idea what a burger was and wanted to try one. The smell of onions and meat and things she couldn't identify greeted her when she pushed open the glass door of the diner. She hoisted herself up on a red leather stool, her feet dangled, and her chest barely cleared grey slick counter.

Betty was stitched on the pink dress of the woman behind the counter. "Shouldn't you be in school, young man?"

Grancie tugged on her jacket, grateful she had dressed in boy's clothes and deepened her voice, "I have completed my studies."

Betty shook her head. "Sure you have. What can I getcha, Hon?"

Grancie pulled the menu from the holder and pointed to the picture of the hamburger. "I want this."

Betty nodded and said. "Whatcha drinkin', Hon?"

Grancie pointed to another item. "Coca Cola, please."

A minute later Betty put the glass of Coke in front of Grancie, who cautiously sipped, her brown eyes widening. "It tingles and is so sweet. Marvelous." She drank the glass empty and asked for more. The Olympic belch that followed made Grancie giggle.

Betty set a thick white plate in front of her. Grancie lifted the fluffy white top and used her fork to move the greenery and tomatoes, exposing the meat. It didn't look like any ham she had ever seen before. She poked it with her fork, picked off a piece, smelled it, stuck it in her mouth, and chewed slowly. Perhaps bovine, chopped fine.

"I've never seen anyone examine a hamburger that closely."

Grancie glanced at the man that sat a couple of stools away. She almost choked as she tried to swallow the bite too quickly. She felt a hand on her back and looked up into blue eyes.

"Sorry, didn't mean to catch you up like that."

He was a dwarf and blond. There were no blond dwarves, only blond elves or faeries. She swallowed. "I was so involved with my meal I did not see you."

"Are you all right now?" He sat down next to her, and Betty moved his plate and twitched an eyelid.

"Yes." Grancie wondered why Betty did that.

"I'm Harvard Williams but call me Billy. Harvard is too pretentious for a midget like me. Are you here for the movie?"

"I do not think so. What is a movie?" Grancie said. She bit into a sliver of crisp fried potato that came with her hamburger. They were so good she couldn't stop eating them.

"Don't let me keep you from your fries." Billy forked a bite of his meal and chewed.

Grancie reassembled her burger and took a bite. With all the pieces together, it was large and delicious. She took another bite, savoring the mix of flavors.

Billy said, "You really don't know what a movie is? You're not from around here then."

He would never believe her. Grancie chewed her hamburger, nibbled potato sticks, and sipped the heady Coca Cola. She had no idea
what to say to the blue-eyed man.

Billy ate and talked. He didn't require a response except from Betty
when he pushed his coffee cup towards her. "Oh, that was the best
meatloaf I've had in a long time." He leaned back and watched Grancie.
"So, young fella, you never told me your name."

Grancie wiped her mouth with the paper napkin and placed it on
the plate like Billy had. "My name is Grancie." She avoided looking directly at Billy even though she knew he stared at her.

"So Grancie, that's an unusual name. Aren't you a little young to be
hanging out at a diner in the middle of the day? Shouldn't you be in
school or something?"

"Oh, he's done with school," Betty said. "What school was that?"

"I am old enough to be here without a chaperone." It was almost as
bad as being home.

Betty laughed and cleared their plates. She slapped their tickets
down in front of them and walked off.

Billy grabbed Grancie's ticket. "Let me get that for you since you're
new in town."

Grancie watched Billy pull green paper from a piece of folded
leather. "Where you heading to now?"

"I will walk somewhere." She wasn't sure she should tell him that.
But she liked him and the way he prattled on.

"Why don't you let me show you some of the sights? I've been here
a couple of weeks now and know my way around pretty good."

His eyes sparkled and she felt a connection she didn't understand.
She nodded.

They walked along Sunset Boulevard for a few minutes before Billy
said, "Why are you dressed as a boy?"

Grancie had hoped her disguise was better than that. "Why do you
say that?"

"Look, you have no beard, no Adam's apple, your hands are delicate, and your voice is feminine."

Grancie stopped and blurted, "Too many people ask if I am lost or need help when I dress as a female. So I go as a male."

"Good reason," Billy said. He took her hand and pulled her along. "Let's go to the studio. I bet they could use you in the cast. Don't you want to be in pictures?"

Pictures? Someone was going to draw her?

"I do not know," Grancie said.

"We'll catch a movie later. Let's go to MGM and sign you up for an interview. We're going to be Munchkins in the Land of Oz."

Grancie's magic enabled her to understand and speak English, but she didn't understand most of what she heard in the cramped offices of the movie studio. Billy told her what to say and helped her fill out the paperwork. A woman with blond hair piled high on her head said to come back in three days for a costume fit. Grancie nodded but didn't think she would be here in three days.

Billy took her to see *Captain Courageous* at the Hollywood Theater. The seats were thickly padded and the room was hushed as the lights lowered. Grancie gasped as images moved across the huge flat surface and music filled the cavernous room. She was enthralled at this human magic and didn't pull away when Billy took her hand. His finger drew lazy circles in her palm. She liked the way that felt.

By the time they walked out of the building tears dampened the corners of her eyes. "That was such a wonderful story. Isn't it fabulous that the boy and his father found each other?"

"Yeah, a regular fairy tale. Hey, where are you staying?" Billy said.

"I was going to return to...." She was about to say Abollar, her home. "I am not sure. Perhaps you can suggest some place?"

Billy almost skipped. "You can get all dolled up, then we can have dinner together and maybe go out to a club afterwards. We'll find you a place to stay."

Grancie knew her boy's clothes weren't proper. She had noticed all the women wore dresses, heeled shoes, fancy hats, and gloves. "I don't have women's clothing."

Billy paused before saying, "I don't know nothin' about women's clothes." He walked around in a circle then snapped his fingers. "There's a dress shop in the next block. Let's go there."

Thirty minutes later Grancie and Billy left the shop carrying two packages and her boy's clothes. She wore a navy skirt, a white blouse with pearly buttons, and black high heeled shoes. Freda and Lizzie, the clerks, had done her long hair in a chignon and applied makeup to her eyes and lips.

"Wow, girly, you look gorgeous," Billy said. "Listen, my place is six or seven blocks from here. Can you walk that far in those shoes?"

She wasn't sure she could, the heels were awkward and unsteady. "Why do you want to go to your apartment?"

"You need to put those packages somewhere and I can call a cab from there. The boarding house has a telephone."

"That might be a good idea. We can walk slow, all right?" Grancie said wondering what a telephone was. She walked all the way without getting a blister or turning an ankle but decided women's shoes were not practical.

Billy's apartment was very small, like the houses of her village. There was a central room with a bed shoved in the corner and a tiny kitchen off in a nook to one side. A door led to the bathroom and another door hid a closet, Billy told her. She set her packages on the floor next to the door.

"Do you want something to drink?" Billy asked.

"Water, please." Grancie wondered if they had mead. She stood by the door, tugging at the tendril of hair that had come loose.

"Have a seat on the divan. I'll bring you a glass of water in a minute."

What was she doing here? Being alone with a man was inappropriate but exciting. She sat stiffly on the edge of the firm but comfortable divan. It was much nicer than the one at home. She watched Billy as he filled the glasses with water. He was the nicest looking man she had ever seen even with his short bowed legs and stocky body. Her race was small by human terms, but everything was sized proportionately.

Billy set the glasses on the table in front of them and sat down next to her. He leaned back and ran his hand down her back. Grancie shivered. The touch was so light she wasn't sure it actually happened until he did it again. She took a drink of her water, held the glass a moment, took another drink, and set it down. His hand pressed more firmly to her back. Warmth flowed from his fingers onto her skin even through the thin fabric of her blouse and camisole. His fingers curled around her side, and he pulled her closer to him.

"Billy, what? I am not... I do not know."

"Ah, Grancie. You are so beautiful. I won't hurt you, I promise."

She felt his fingers brush across her breast and felt tingly warmth creep through her body. She leaned into him. His fingers barely reached the side of her breast but it was like lightning to her soul. She turned her face to him. Those eyes, those beautiful blue eyes seemed to grow larger until she wanted to crawl into them.

He leaned closer until their lips touched. Her breath caught, she was suffocating, her eyes closed and rolled back in her head. Was it always like this? She pulled away, opened her eyes to look at him then pulled him to her, fastening her lips to his, trying to weld them together with the heat flowing through her body. Billy pulled her chignon loose and held on as if the winds of Olympus had begun to blow. His other hand stroked her breast and Grancie felt her nipples rise and harden like the silver and gold her family mined. His lips moved to her chin, over to her ear lobe. She could feel his soft breath in her ear and she shuddered. His lips moved down her neck, back across to the hollow in her throat, his hand still gripped her hair pulling her head back. His lips made their way back up to hers and fastened on them. He pushed his tongue between her teeth and she bit the invading flesh.

"Ow. What'd you do that for?"

"I need to breathe." Grancie shook her head. She was not in Abollar. Billy would never come to Abollar and no one would know about him. Why should she not enjoy this time with him? Is this not what she came here for, to see how other people lived and enjoy the freedom? She took his hand and placed it on her breast. He squeezed and slipped his fingers to the nipple and rolled it between his thumb and forefinger until she moaned. Nothing felt like this with the fumblings of the boy in her world. She wanted more. There should be more.

He took his fingers off her breast long enough to unbutton her blouse and tug it out of her skirt. He looked at the fine silk camisole as if he'd never seen one before. He touched the fabric then ran his hand over her breasts. Grancie felt both her nipples respond and the dampness between her legs spread.

"This feels incredible. What is this?" Billy kept his fingers moving between her breasts, letting them slide over the silk.

"What?" Grancie mumbled. Her eyes were closed and she didn't want to open them.

"This slip you're wearing. It feels like heaven with your titties so tight under it." Billy pulled his arm out from behind her and leaned over to bite at her nipples. His hand found its way down her lap and Grancie had a new shiver sliding up her belly.

Grancie reached over and placed a hand on Billy's chest. It was solid under her fingers. She let them explore, felt his tiny nubby nipples and stroked them until they hardened. She wondered if that felt as good to him as it did for her. She unbuttoned his shirt and found he wore a stretchy coarse undershirt that she tugged out of his pants. She ran her hand across his bare skin and felt the small hairs on his chest. She worked her way down to the top of his slacks. He inhaled sharply.

"This is fair treatment," Grancie whispered in his ear. His hands played with the top of her stocking and she felt him unhook the garter.

When his hand went further, she forgot all about where her hand was. The fire burned and she wanted more.

Billy pulled her off the divan and led her to the bed tucked into the corner. The blue flowered chintz bedspread looked well washed and soft. Why did she notice that? His hands pulled her stockings down slowly, taking care with the delicate material. Fingers brushed her calves and ankles and the ticklish place on her foot. He placed the stockings on a chair then pulled her to him, planted his lips on hers while his hands found the button in the back of her skirt. By the time the kiss finished, Grancie stood in her slip and camisole.

"My God, you're so beautiful." Billy said and pulled her to him again, kissing her, thrusting his tongue between her lips.

She explored the intruder with the tip of her own tongue and found it responsive. Their tongues danced and played together while hands stroked and squeezed. Grancie could no more think than she could tap dance. She pushed Billy's shirt off his shoulders and grabbed his undershirt, tugging it up and over his head, only breaking the contact with his lips long enough to clear the material from his head. His blond hair brushed her forehead. It felt like feathers. Her fingers found his belt and she unbuckled it and let it hang loose in the belt loops. She managed the top button of his slacks, but zippers were not common in Abollar and she couldn't quite... his hands found hers and helped tug the zipper down and his trousers fell away.

Grancie pushed Billy away. She wanted to see him without trappings. She had seen her brothers in various stages of dress, but they were her brothers and it was not the same. Tight blond curls covered his broad chest and his green striped shorts tented in front. She reached out to touch the bulge, but he stepped back.

"If you touch me now, I won't last two seconds."

Grancie did not understand but stopped. Billy pulled the camisole over her head. He bent over and licked her nipples while he tugged her slip and panties off. She stepped out of them and he pushed her on the bed. As he crawled over her, she felt his need. He pulled her up closer to him and kissed the top of her forehead, kissed her eyelids, moved to her lips where he lingered. She wrapped her arms around him until he wiggled. He kissed his way down her chin and neck. His lips played between her breasts, making fire kindle in her belly. He moved lower. His fingers tapped through the curly hair between her legs and she spread them.

Billy scooted down the bed, touching her in intimate places. Grancie's eyes popped open when she felt his head between her legs, and then she forgot everything except the intense waves of pleasure. She gripped the old iron headboard and thrust her hips into his face. She could hear his muffled laugh and she pushed against him again. Every place he touched her flamed and started waves of sensation that coursed through her to the core of her body. She moved faster and the pleasure built until it exploded out of her in a cloud of pinks and purples and blues.

Billy shifted and she felt a quick flash of pain before she realized he was inside her, filling her with more sensations. She moved against him and grabbed his ass. He thrust into her for only a moment before he shuddered and slowed, and she opened her eyes to see him staring at her in wonder. "What was that with all the colors? My God, it was like nothing I've ever seen or felt before." He lowered himself to rest on his elbows and his body pressed her into the mattress.

"What did you see?" Grancie felt limp and wonderful. Purple and blue still colored her mind.

"I saw colors like a rainbow." He reached up as if to grab something from the air but his hand remained empty. "Just my imagination, I guess." He rolled off her and pulled her close.

Grancie snuggled against him, wanting the connection now as much as before. "I saw the rainbow too. It was wonderful." She shifted so she faced him and wondered why he was dwarf sized instead of regular human sized. How do you ask such a question? In Abollar it was rude to ask people why they were different. Her stomach made gurgling noises.

"You're hungry. I forgot." Billy struggled to get up, but Grancie was hungry for something else.

"No, I am all right. I just want to stay here." She ran her finger down his chest, making slow circles in the damp curly hair. Her finger moved further south until it tangled in the stickiness left by their love making. Like magic a soft lump of flesh transformed into a rigid shaft. She touched it and explored the roundness and further to the furry sacks that tightened as she stroked. Her finger could barely reach around this wonder. She moved her hand up the shaft and down and smiled as Billy groaned.

Grancie felt her own response to him even without his touch. She crawled on top of him and slid him into her, rocking back and forth. He filled her completely and she gave way to the rush of pleasure.

Billy grabbed her hips and stroked into her over and over again until colors of pink and red that faded to orange then green and blue filled her mind. A touch of purple burst behind her eyes and her body shuddered. He pulled her down to him and kissed her until she felt her lips were not her own.

"My God woman, how do you do that?"

"What?" Grancie did not care what she did. It did not matter right now.

"Make those rainbows," Billy said. He wrapped his arms around her and held her until she pushed herself off of him.

"Um, I need to go...." She glided to the toilet without thinking about covering her naked body.

The bathroom was a wonder because the waste was flushed out somewhere and didn't stink. The tub gleamed white and water flowed out of the spigot. She pushed a plug in the hole and let the vessel fill with water. Life here was easy, so easy.

She soaked until the water started to cool and she let all the lovely water drain away. Billy was asleep when she emerged from her ablution. He was so cute with his soft snores.

Grancie gathered her borrowed clothing, folded them in a neat pile, and left them on the divan. She pulled her boy's clothes out of the package and put them on, leaving the boots for last. After looking around a bit, she found a pencil and paper and wrote Billy a note.

Thank you Harvard Williams.

She carried her boots and put them on outside. The sun had set, but there were so many lights from the city, Grancie had no trouble finding her way back to the road that led to where she had entered this world. She pulled out the magic book and mouthed the words. Maybe she would come back. She could be in pictures.

Ash and Elm

by Bess Lyre

THE FIRST MAN WAS MADE from an ash tree and his wife was made from an elm.

Yet it is not a man's axe that rings like a bell in the constant winter-darkness, setting a distant tree to shrieking in a language that only dryads and alder tree girls can hear. Nor is the axe a woman's.

A dwarf has come to my forested isle, seeking magical fuel for forge fires that imbue weapons with power.

Help us, alder tree girl, the dryads cry. *Help us.*

They cannot leave their trees in the night, but I can. I slip from the safety of its gnarled, medicinal, lichen-covered trunk and patter along the catkin-scattered bridge of snow that connects my alder tree's grey, granite pedestal to the main part of the island.

Dryad voices, like wind in leaves, guide me to the deepest part of the forest. There, monumental ash trees that have stood since the beginning form cathedrals to block out the light of the stars.

And there is the dwarf. I smell his sweat- and snow-damp ringlets, the dwarf-musk of him. I can all but taste his tongue. I don't need starlight to see him with my wide owl-eyes. His silver axe has barely broken through the bark of the greatest and oldest ash tree.

White wolf furs and leather defend him from the cold, but he has set his coat against a moss-covered stone to give freedom to his well-muscled arms. His hands on the axe-haft are fine and strong.

This will be no difficult task, I sing to the dryads, slipping my own moon-white cloak from my shoulders and loosening my braid over bare skin. *It will be a pleasure to distract this impertinent little man.* To dance away with him to the icy water's edge and then drown him, so he might never again threaten the forest.

I move out of the deep shadows and into the corner of his field of view.

The axe freezes, mid-swing. The dwarf's head jerks upward and his nostrils flare. His face is younger than I expected, his long-lashed eyes dark and shining. His black beard is short and tidy, leaving his cheeks bare, and on one of those smooth cheeks, the symbol of a forge-hammer glows as though coals have been set inside of it.

I miss a step, startled. He is branded by the gods.

This dwarf is no woodcutter, but one of the sons of Ivaldi. Renowned smiths and jewellers, they dare to craft Thor and Odin's playthings; they can survive the whims of the immortals but not the direct rays of the sun.

"Have you no mercy for that old fellow?" I ask, still stepping sidelong to prevent him from focusing on me, moving neither closer nor further away. It is a good technique for befuddling men; unfortunately, dwarves see keenly in the dark.

"He shall serve the needs of the god Freyr," the dwarf answers, the axe still half-raised.

"Your reach is short. Summer may come before you finish the mighty task of severing him from the ground."

"Then you had best leave me to it."

"What is your name?" I give him my best seductive smile, but he is wary. I make sure that my back remains hidden, that my leaf-green breasts point toward him.

"Why should I give you that power over me?"

Rune, the trees sigh. *His name is Rune.*

"I am twice your height, Rune, Ivaldi's son," I say. "I already have power over you."

And I stop moving, at last.

His eyes fall from my face to my body and his mouth falls open, just a little. Name-magic is for the gods. Not for alder tree girls. Still, I have never failed to lead a man away from the tree he was intent on butchering.

He is not a man, the dryads remind me.

"I know what you are," Rune says. "If you don't go away, I'll find your tree and chop it down instead."

Quicker than his eyes can follow, I flit behind the ash tree he has injured, peer around it and hold my cold fingers out to him.

"Come with me," I whisper. "I'll show it to you."

His smell surrounds me. I have no scent of my own. Even the juices between my thighs, when they flow—as they flow, now, in proximity to hot blood, hot flesh—run clear and sweet as springwater.

In that moment, the trees scream, *Fire! Fire!*

Elsewhere in the forest, heat blossoms. I feel the dread, the danger of it, in my core.

"Something is wrong," the dwarf surmises, looking into my stricken face. My fingers have fallen away from him. "What does the forest tell you?"

I press both hands to my chest, where no heart beats.

"It tells me that two warriors have sailed to the isle to escape from Moongarm. But the giant wolf has swum across the lake in pursuit of them. They have lit a fire to try and keep the wolf at bay."

Then I have no more time for Rune, son of Ivaldi. With clumsiness born of haste, I crash through the woods, heavy as a human woman. As I approach the island's edge, the place where my tree lies on its little outcropping, I smell the smoke, and the wild, old-blood smell of Moongarm.

The fire is out. The flames have been quenched by the padding of giant paws. The wolf towers over the black shape of the longboat beached on the shore, but he is not quite tall enough, even on his back legs, to reach the puny humans who have scaled a twenty-metre-tall elm and now cling to its shuddering branches.

Moongarm will knock me down, the dryad inside the elm sobs.

He cannot, the other dryads reassure her. *Your roots are deep. Moongarm can only kill you if you leave the safety of your tree.*

I stand there, gaping at the beast as it turns its ferocious gaze from the trapped warriors to me.

I can be killed. I have left the safety of my tree. And there is no way for me to get back to it without getting past the great wolf. Unable to reach his prey, he leaps toward me, teeth gnashing in anticipation; each tooth is as big as Rune's axe and wetly gleaming.

Flying through the trees like dead leaves on the wind, I am supernaturally fast, but so is the wolf. I reach the heart of the forest slightly ahead of Moongarm. I can hear him thrashing, caught by root tangles and slipping on moss, but he will catch up to me, soon.

The dwarf, Rune, catches my wrist.

"Does the fire spread?"

His face is frowning. Serious. He does not look at my back. He does not look at the place where the inside surface of my ribs forms an empty cage. Alder tree girls have no spine. No lungs. No heart, to be betrayed by.

"It's Moongarm," I gasp, just as the giant wolf skids angrily into the clearing. It snarls at the dwarf, the ruff of fur on the back of its neck erecting like a forest of icicles.

"Ah," Rune says. He releases my wrist.

Then, he takes a hammer from his belt, strides forward and strikes the wolf in the nose.

There are red sparks, as though the dwarf has struck a red-hot blade. Moongarm howls. He thrashes. He slips his white muzzle sideways to try to snap his jaw shut around the dwarf's legs, but the hammer comes down on his nose again.

More sparks, and brighter.

"Stay back from me, old fellow," Rune cries as he strikes the wolf a third time. "Stay back from my smell. Or I shall be the last thing you ever smell."

Moongarm turns. His haunches bunch and quiver. Rune strikes him a fourth time, in the arse, just as the great wolf springs away.

When the light from the dying sparks is gone, I find that I am sprawled in the moist earth of the forest floor, my fingers dug into my face, and that Rune is looking down at me, smiling grimly.

"There. Now I have saved your life."

"Yes," I say.

"Will you do me the courtesy of not trying to drown me, then?"

"I won't try to drown you."

He laughs at himself. Shakes his head slightly. As if the promise of an alder tree girl can be trusted.

"Look. I'm going back to work, now. Stay and watch, if you can bear to watch. Moongarm won't bother you here. But don't try to touch me. You'll regret it if you do."

He replaces the hammer at his belt. He picks up the axe again. The dryad in the tree screams at the bite of the blade.

Shaking, I get carefully to my feet. I brush myself down. If I cannot touch the dwarf, then I must distract him from his wicked work with words.

"Why this tree? Why this island? The sons of Ivaldi have never come here before."

Rune answers without pausing in his swing.

"The trees are close to the water. This tree will be a ship. Skidbladnir will be its name. It will sail against the wind, to wherever the gods command. When it reaches its destination, it will fold like a map and fit into a pocket."

"That cannot be!"

"I will make it so. My brothers and I. They will come when the wood is dried and seasoned."

I wince. He speaks of the bones of a living creature.

"The gods are greedy. Can they not already travel wherever they wish?"

"You mourn for your friend," Rune grunts. "But soon he, who has been rooted to this place, will travel with them."

MOONGARM STAYS ON THE island, beneath the elm tree, waiting for the warrior-fruit to fall.

I stay with Rune, watching him, not touching him. It has been three days. Three days away from my tree, and I begin to die as surely as if Moongarm had caught me in his hungry maw.

My skin fades from green to golden brown. My full flesh begins to sag.

Even in the darkness, Rune notices.

"You look poorly, alder tree girl," he says, looking up from the coals where he warms his mead.

"Do you care?"

"It is not your tree that I came for. I have finished all the felling that I intend to do here."

The spirit of the ash tree is faded forever. His voice is silent, though the sap still weeps from the lengths of green wood that the dwarf has split into manageable lengths.

"So you only kill when it is necessary?"

"Yes."

"Then kill Moongarm!"

"I will not leave this clearing. Not until my brothers come. I know what you forest folk are like. You would hide the dead wood, to punish me. You would sink it into the lake or bury it in the earth. You would ruin it, simply to deny me."

Yesssss, the dryads hiss furiously. *Oh, yesss, we would.*

"If you don't kill Moongarm, I will die."

"If I don't build the ship I will be punished by the gods. Punishments so severe you could scarcely imagine them."

"Then hold me while I fade," I implore him. "I am so cold."

"No." He stares into the dying embers of his fire.

"I'm afraid of death, of nothingness. Hold me, please."

"How many men and dwarves have you drowned?"

I have never drowned a dwarf, but I do not say it. Instead, I say, "The ash cannot be restored to life. There would be no point in drowning you now." I flex my fingers. They are so numb that I can barely feel them. The fingernails are grey and split like old leaves lashed by the bitter wind.

"Perhaps you could not," Rune allows softly. "Perhaps you are too weak."

My teeth chatter.

"It is inside me," I say, kneeling abruptly beside him, so that we are eye to eye. He does not flinch. "Cold wind where my heart should be. Hold me from behind. Close the space. Keep it warm until I'm faded."

He sighs. The fire goes dark. Only the brand on his cheek still burns.

"Turn around," he says, setting his mead to one side.

I turn. Without my cloak drawn over my shoulders, he has no choice but to stare into my vacant, organ-less chest cavity, but when he speaks again his voice contains no trace of horror.

"Lean back."

Awkwardly, I shift my weight, from being on my knees to squatting, then falling backward. It is a short fall, into white wolf fur and leather. He smells of snow and sweat and honey and dwarf and ash.

"You are very light," he says, shifting me a little. This time, his voice is husky. I feel the swollen organ beneath his woollen britches, short and fat as a turnip, and the sweet sap in my cleft beginning its slow seep.

"I am almost gone," I whisper. "A few more hours."

"You have no woman's heart, but you have a woman's parts," he says, his smith's hands smearing my breasts. "That is a severe punishment, worthy of the gods."

"I have all the women's parts I need."

His fingers dip into my sap. His breathing deepens as he tastes it. His beard scratches against my right side as his powerful arms squeeze me again, and then I'm being lifted by the buttocks; he's so strong; and I am light, as he said; and he's holding me over his head like a chalice and lapping from the cleft between my legs while my fingers and toes touch the leaf litter and my back arches between them.

I make a small cry as we roll back together and his tongue touches the hard bud hidden there. He's on his back in the mulch, now, and I'm sitting on his face. The jolt of sensation strikes again, and again, until I'm half-delirious with it. While his mouth works on me, hot against cold, I unlace his wolf fur and leather vest, finding sheathed knives and woollens underneath.

His stocky body tenses as I draw one of the knives. Like his cheek, the silver blade is marked with a glowing brand. His tongue falters, but he does not throw me off. I could kill him.

I don't kill him. I cut away his woollen shirt, trousers, and drawers.

Cold air swirls through the inside of my chest. I'm still dying but this is a good way to die; Rune's four fingers sliding in and out of me.

I drop the knife in the leaf litter. Throw my head back and silently sing as orgasm convulses me. At full strength, my woody innards might have broken Rune's fingers. As it is, he is trapped uncomfortably for a moment, then freed.

When my head droops I see his hairy, sculpted chest and muscled belly with its trail of curls beneath me. From the black nest of his pubic hair, the eye of his stumpy, pale penis glistens with a single bead; it smears like warm mead over the head when I press my thumb to it.

"You are supposed to be keeping me warm from behind," I whisper. I bow down on my knees with my forehead to the soil and he pulls himself out from under me. For a moment, I am alone, a cold, dying alder tree girl beside the bones of an ancient ash, and then he joins me again, plunging his penis into a hole whose tightness I control, trapping him voluntarily now as I trapped him involuntarily before. His hips buck and he comes quietly and almost instantly.

"Keep holding me," I say into the starlit silence. With a slow sigh, he obeys.

Once he is sleeping, I stir.

I stretch, still weak; so weak, but the inside of my chest holds a little warmth lent by the dwarf.

Rune. It glows on his cheek. The mark of the hammer so feared by the giant wolf, Moongarm.

Kill him! the dryads cry. *Kill him while he sleeps!*

No, I sing back to them. *I will not kill him. He is leaving. He will take his boat and he will leave.*

Instead of reaching for Rune's axe, I walk fearlessly through the forest, towards the rocky outcropping where my tree waits for me. Moongarm's ferocious bulk lies between us, but I am safe from Moongarm, now.

Stay back from my smell, Rune had told the monstrous beast, *or I shall be the last thing you ever smell.*

Moongarm, snarling and with his fluffy hide bristling, retreats from my smell. I smell of Rune's sweat and his semen. I smell of snow and honey and ash.

Wizard's Staff

by Julie Cox

NEXT TO BORABI, I WAS short. Not that I was tall next to most other people, either, but Borabi's long limbs were a dramatic contrast to my stocky build. He was lithe and graceful until he was startled, then those limbs went flailing everywhere like a colt's. When that happened, I laughed, and he scowled. Most of the time it was the other way around.

Like now. He writhed beneath me, a squirming mess of an elf, his breath hitching as he tried to stop himself from laughing. I held the paintbrush away from him and cuffed his pointed ear.

"Stop moving," I said. "These runes are very precise. I don't want to open a portal to some demonic realm because you're ticklish."

"I can't help it, Shale," he lied.

He could help it very well. He had unbelievable control, when he chose to exercise it. I leaned close over him, dabbing a spot of cornflower blue paint on his delicate nose. "Hold still, or I will stop touching you."

His pretty hazel eyes fluttered wide and his body stilled beneath me.

"There now," I crooned, "that's better." I drew the paint in thin lines across his body, weaving a spell with interlocking runes, the language of dwarves and of magic. I traced the curve of his bicep with a rune for the sorceress I needed to contact. His other arm was wreathed in the symbols of magical power, symbols for me to draw upon, like sinking a

39

well into the ground beneath us to pull up the magic of the earth. I was dwarven; my magic was the power of stone and wells and mines and old language. I'd covered his chest in the runes of our families, the significant runes of our lives, the collective language that described our lives, apart and together. In naming them, I named us. We were the sum of our stories—literally, in the case of runic magic. Those had been easy; I'd painted those a thousand times.

I slid down his half-nude body, careful not to smudge the runes. I knelt between his legs and undid the lacing on his pants. He grinned at me, and I gave him a warning look: don't move. He bit his lip and obeyed. We'd been together long enough I could command him by raising an eyebrow, curling a lip, crooking a finger. Of course, he disobeyed half the time, all mischief and playfulness, so that I would have to engage him and correct him. Neither of us would have it any other way.

He was half hard already as I pulled his pants down and away. He purred little groans and moans as I stroked the paintbrush up the underside of his cock, the cool slickness of the paint contrasting the heat of his skin and the callouses of my hand. He was long and slender, whereas I was short and thick. Just like we were everywhere else. His balls were hairless; a pale patch of straight, silky-soft hair fringed his crotch, as blonde as he was everywhere else. The paint eased the friction as I ran my hand up and down his cock, the head emerging from his foreskin as he stiffened.

I lowered my mouth to his cock and slid it between my lips. I felt the blood swell his cock in my mouth, growing more turgid every moment. He tasted salty and distinctly elven, like rain and grass and the damp forest floor. The paint was sweet, and as familiar a taste as his skin. He rocked his hips, wanting more, trying to fuck my mouth. I rasped my tongue against the underside of his cock, right where he liked it. That got him to stop moving, though he grew distinctly louder, and the rest of him began to squirm again.

My own cock was hard now, and my body begged for friction. I sat up and undid my own pants. I raised his narrow hips and pressed between his thighs, grasping us both in one thick-fingered hand.

"Shale," he whispered, letting his head fall back. I loved the shape of my name in his mouth. He made it sound like something beautiful and ephemeral, instead of a flaky rock.

"Oh my stars, you're so gorgeous," I rasped, watching him writhe in pleasure. "Sometimes I'm astounded you picked me. How'd I get so lucky?"

"S'not luck," he said with a lecherous smirk. "It was dogged persistence. On *my* part. Or have you forgotten me howling outside your window like a fox in heat?"

"I don't think anyone who heard it ever forgot that," I said. God he felt good, and the memory of him professing his adoration for me so many years ago got me going all the more. I could stroke us off in moments; I knew exactly how to hold us together, how fast to go, how hard to squeeze. I knew the steps to this dance so well. But we weren't at that kind of ball.

He made a pitiful little noise of disappointment as I drew away from him, wiped the paint from his cock, and reloaded the paint brush. He jerked ever so slightly when I spiraled the blue paint over his balls, up his cock. It was cold against his now fever-hot skin, and he wilted a little. I dabbed a bit on the pad of my finger and slid it against his ass, pleasuring him that way, to get him back to full rigidity. I needed him as hard as he could get for this part, but I couldn't touch his cock anymore, not with the paint spiral on him. I slid a finger inside him; he unclenched, and I read the concentration on his suddenly serious face as he willed himself to relax. I added more paint, slicking my fingers; I applied a generous smear to my own cock, and he bit his lower lip, spread his legs wider.

"C'mon, Shale," he said. "I can take it."

"Whether you can or not is not the question," I said. "I need you to stay completely rigid, and that means I will not skirt the edge between pleasure and pain, or think of my own pleasure first. I must only inflict pleasure upon you this time, love."

"Poor me," he said. He let his head fall back as I pushed two fingers into him. My short, thick digits together were as large as an elf's cock, and Borobi slid ever so slightly back and forth on the stone floor, fucking himself on my hand. I put my other hand on his hip and held him, or tried to.

"I don't want to scratch up that pretty back," I said to him. I scissored my fingers, stretching him, then turned my hand, pushed as far in as I could, and began stroking that little spot in front that made his every muscle twitch with exquisite pleasure. I went slowly, gently, not wanting to bring him too soon and ground out the spell I'd written upon him. He moaned, his syllables incomprehensible. He tried to take his cock in hand and I swatted it away.

"I want to come," he whined.

"And you will. But not yet. I need you first."

He flattened his knees to the side. "Will you enter me at least?"

I removed my fingers, smiled, and leaned over him, the head of my paint-wet cock pressed against his ass. "Tell me what you want. Explicit, detailed, or I'll not fuck you at all. I can finished the spell without either of us actually coming."

"Don't you dare," he snarled.

"There's my wild elf. C'mon. You suck my cock with that mouth, so use it."

His expression was halfway between a grin and a snarl. "I want you to penetrate me," he said. "I want you to push your cock up my ass. I want you to fuck me hard, make me feel it. I want you to mark me and claim me and own me and master me. Show me who's boss, Shale."

The fact of the matter was that Borabi was the boss, but he didn't seem to know that. Everything I did waited on him. I prepped him, and waited for him to tell me I could enter him. I gathered the magic, worked and forged it, and he told me where and why to use it. I held him down, tied him up, when he told me he needed it and wanted it—which he never did out loud, naturally. That would be too easy on me. No, I had to watch for the patterns in speech and gesture for him to tell me what he wanted. It took a lot of work to be Borabi's lover.

But he was worth it. I pressed the head of my cock against the puckered ring of his ass and rocked my hips forward, penetrating his flesh. He moaned and shivered. I went little by little, two nudges forward, one nudge back, until I was balls-deep in him and he was so tight and hot around me it almost hurt. I pulled back out, almost all the way, added more of that cool, wet paint, and shoved back into him. He grinned maniacally. He loved this part, loved the initial sheathing, when he was so tight I could barely stand it and could barely resist it.

"I have to do the spell," I managed to say.

"Fine, go ahead with your spell," he said, head lolling back. "Just don't stop moving in me, ok?"

I held a shaking hand out, fingers spread, and murmured low in the old language of stone and water and magic. The blue paint began to glow. Across his chest and shoulders, on the tip of his nose, he glowed, eerie and beautiful, magic lighting up the runic paint. The spiral up his cock glowed. My cock glowed, visible then not visible from one moment to the next, dripping down my balls as I pumped into my lover. The magic liked that. Magic liked obscene acts, naked and primal ruttings in the dark. It liked secrets, and secret spaces, and raw, intimate moments. There was a reason witches danced naked by the fire, and why sex magic was so effective.

A portal opened in front of me, a gateway between us and the sorceress I sought. The sorceress that had dropped us into this cave, this prison. She started as she met my eyes through the gateway.

"What—How—?" She recovered quickly. "Clever creature, you've summoned a speaking-glass spell. How you did it with no wizard's staff is beyond me." She gave me a demure smile. "You must tell me your secrets when I call upon you later."

"Anything long and hard can substitute for a wizard's staff," I said. No need to get explicit yet about what long, hard objects I was using for a staff. "Allow me finish the message I'd set out to give you when you dropped my elvish friend and I into your dungeon." I rocked in and out of said elvish friend, and he looked smug about it.

"The pretty blonde creature? Oh, tell me you sacrificed him to a dark god!" Her smile was inhuman, her eyes rimmed with white.

"Oh, he's taken a pounding," I said, and Borabi sat up on his elbows to give me a 'what are you thinking?' look. He had a point. In my defense, my brain was low on blood.

She wasted only a moment trying to puzzle out what I was talking about before chasing the thought away with a little toss of her head and returning to the most pressing matter at hand. "You've gone to such trouble to deliver a message, so deliver it."

I unscrewed the back end of the paintbrush and poured the tiny mountain of gold dust into my palm. I puffed up my cheeks and blew a straight, hard wind across my hand, carrying the dust through the gateway. The sorceress shook her head in surprise, blinking as the dust settled across her face.

"What is this magic?" she shrieked. "What can cross a speaking-glass? Have you cursed me, you foul creature, I'll—"

I was having some trouble talking while keeping up with Borabi, who had taken to shifting back and forth, fucking himself upon my cock when I faltered at maintaining a rhythm. Impatient man. I let her spew vile insults at me while I regained my control, hissing at Borabi that I couldn't finish yet, he had to slow down. He grinned at me like a teenager getting away with something.

"It's gold dust, is all," I said at last, interrupting her.

She stopped. "Gold dust? Why...?"

"Ground from a ring, from the hand of the Yellow King," I said.

She snarled. "That traitorous—"

"Oh, she speaks of traitors!" I said to Borabi, who wriggled his hips in a circle, making me bite my lip to keep from crying out. I focused on the sorceress. "And here I thought it was you who stole his treasure, made off with his child in the dead of night, when you were supposed to be married the next day."

She made a face. "It was more complex than that."

"It usually is." Borabi clenched and unclenched on me in light flutters, making me gasp and my eyes water.

"It was my dowry in the first place, and his child? Please, she was twenty years old, she was no more a child than you are." Understanding lit her face. "Are you doing something obscene over there?"

"Absolutely I am. And what did the king vow?"

"That he would give me a ring, and thus claim me, and I—" she stopped. "The ground up dust of a ring?"

"You can't give it back," I pointed out.

Her beautiful face twisted into a snarl. "You think you've captured me for that fool with a bunch of dust and a speaking-glass spell? It can't end that way! It can't! I've come too far!" She smashed something crystalline beside her; little white shards flew into the air like stars and disappeared.

"It was a complex spell, bound into that ring before it was ground down; it took him this long to work it. Give him some credit. Listen, I—oh wow, you have to stop that, elf—I sympathize with your plight. I'm just the messenger. You could offer to give the treasure back in return for your freedom."

"I already spent it," she muttered.

"On what?"

"Books and tuition."

"That's an expensive education."

"Sorceress," she said, as if that explained everything.

"Give me a second." I drew a line across Borabi's hips and tummy with a thin line of paint, drawing the magic away from the spiral on his cock to the rest of his body. It burned blue like the rest. There, that bought me a little flexibility. I took his cock in my hand and he stopped squirming so much beneath me, breathing hard and fast, his back arching up off the stone ground. For a moment I focused upon his body, the pleasure of sliding in and out of him. He bucked upward, perfectly angled to move along the shaft of my cock and fuck my hand, the glowing paint spreading across his pelvis and balls, getting caught in the light blonde hairs. There, he was happy now. I returned my attention to the sorceress.

"Are you done?" she asked, unimpressed.

"No, but I'm close," I gasped. "But listen. I realize you have me at your mercy."

"Indeed I do," she said.

"Indeed I do," Borabi echoed.

"And I wouldn't have come here if I hadn't had a backup plan."

She rolled her eyes. "Do tempt me with a different sort of cage, a new bargain, little dwarf. I have not yet had my fill of fae nonsense."

First, I was not fae, I was dwarven, there was a huge difference. And second, I was not a *little* dwarf. I was rather tall for a dwarf, and more lithe than most, thanks to a human grandfather. But I didn't have time to parse peculiarities with her. Besides, I had to wrap this up before my "staff" became more of a limp noodle.

"Here me out," I said. "If you think about it a minute, you'll see that the Yellow King made two fatal errors with both his spell and its execution. In the latter, he sent a spellcaster capable of delivering the ring and sealing the magic. But he did not make allowances or plans for getting said spellcaster *out* again."

"He set you up," she said, lifting an eyebrow. "Or didn't even think of your fate long enough to realize it. Selfish prick. So he sent me an ally who knows the spell and its peculiarities."

I nodded. "I don't ordinarily hold with treachery, but I owe no kind of allegiance to he who would send my husband and me off to death or worse without even blinking an eye. After a lifetime of service, too."

She winced "Harsh. Well, he is the Yellow King. Great hoards of gold and all that. He didn't get where he is by caring much about others."

"Exactly. You're just another treasure to him, an object. He wants you because he was denied you once, because you took from him. In his twisted mentality," I amended. "Therefore, the spell he worked on that ring carries that attitude with it. Which brings us to the flaw in the ring's spell. Its specific wording was, you would be bound to give your hand in marriage." I paused in emphasis. "Your *hand*. Now, we all know that's metaphor, but that's the funny thing about magic."

"Its language is open to interpretation." She smirked.

"Yup. The less specific you are, the more the spell can be twisted."

"I'm kind of attached to my hand," she mused, "but more attached to my freedom. And then, dwarves *are* renowned craftsmen."

Borabi scowled and said loudly, "So are elves! I'm the craftsman, he's the magic one!"

"Pardon me," she said. "So, you imply you can make for me a replacement?"

"I'll make you a hand so wondrous you'll consider cutting the other hand off to get a matched set."

She arched a brow. "You'll need to release control of the ring's spell to me, for me to twist its meaning to my purpose."

"Let us out first."

She scoffed. "You invaded my home, attacked me. I have no reason to trust you. You are but words so far. I think a show of faith is more appropriate from you."

"Ok, but I'll have to close the speaking glass as soon as it finishes." As soon as I finished, actually. I looked down at Borabi." "I'm going to need your help on this one."

"Not a problem," he answered coolly. He closed his eyes, concentrating. He squeezed down on me, just a little, so that he could feel every inch of me as I worked in and out of him. His muscles warmed, nearly too hot to be withstood. I gasped, and pumped harder into him out of no volition of my own. He tilted his hips up and down, slowly, changing the angle just a bit with every thrust of my cock. I moaned, jaw slack, my braids falling over the bare skin of my back.

I knew exactly what I needed to send that much magic to her. I withdrew from him suddenly. "Get on all fours," I growled at him, and he grinned. He flipped over, ass in the air, and I may have hurt him a little as I pushed back into him with sudden force. Every movement of my hips hit that spot he liked so much, and he keened in a higher pitched voice. I loved this angle; I was better able to see my cock penetrating him, the light of the blue paint pulsing as I buried my cock in him. I reached around him and grabbed his cock, and began stroking him in rhythm to my own thrusts, as if between us we had a straight line from my balls to the tip of his cock. I solidified in my mind the idea of a wizard's staff, a wizard summoning as much power from his staff as possible, laying out the laws of magic with his rod in hand. As magic would pour from the end of his rod, so it poured from me into him, and from the end of Borabi's cock, onto the ground. I rode him through it, sending magic through the speaking glass, my end of the tether that tied me to the Yellow King's spell. It was sloppy, imprecise magic, spilling out everywhere. The glass closed, the blue light faded out, and I collapsed onto my back, utterly exhausted.

She was kind enough to let us stew for only half a day before she let us out. Downright gracious, for a sorceress. The hand Borabi fashioned for her was, indeed, magnificent, covered in fine filigree like metallic lace. Personally I thought it was a little gawdy, but she loved it. For my part, I frequently thought of the hand she cut off and sent back to the Yellow King. I thought of how his attendant must have screamed (it would have been an attendant, not him personally), and how he must have raged when he discovered his error and my betrayal. The sorceress turned out to have an education worth every penny of her spent fortune, which made her a fascinating (and broke) person. The Yellow King's daughter, against all odds, had better sense, and between her sense and Borabi's craftsman knowledge, they made sure their academic lovers had money for books.

I heard a story once that the hand sits beside him in the Yellow Queen's throne, and he takes it to bed with him. But it's only rumor. Still, it gives me satisfaction to know that his four enemies are safe within the sorceress's tower, finding out all we can about sex magic, and all that powerful villain can get is a hand job. There's a little justice in the world after all.

Cave Dwellers

by Alanna McFall

TO DURWIG
   Of the Clan Stoneforest
   Of the Hall Froststeppe

DEAR COUSIN,

Hello Durwig, greetings from your dear Cousin Thenden! I give you nothing but the best from my travels here. These human lands are a mess, so the best I can give you is none too good, but still I give it to you! Enjoy them as best you can.

Not much has changed since I last wrote to you. I am still travelling with this pack of humans, trying to scope out good positions for joined military bases. Every day it feels like some new piece of stupidity falls out of their mouths (and has a long way to fall before it hits the ground). I tell you, I was always meant to be a soldier, not one of these soft-footed diplomat types they want me to be.

But that is not why I am writing to you, Cousin. I am writing to tell you about the best fuck I have had since I left the homelands, and even longer than that, going back years, decades. I have not felt so alive and full of blood and beer in any sort of memory. The humans are too shirking, too squeamish to hear the story in its full glorious telling, so the words must be relayed to you.

I met the dwarf in question after a "state event," which is never where one expects to find the sort of dwarf you want to meet. Dark, dark skin that shone like good burnished leather and a beard to be proud of, all wiry hair coiled in bands, spreading across their broad chest and matching the same wires on a noble domed head. They were swilling their beer at a human inn and filling the air with smoke and laughter. The humans were so afraid of that laugh they were backing away! But as soon as I heard it, I knew I needed to sate my ears on more.

I sidled up to the bar and got a mug of the best human ale (which raises itself from pathetic to merely terrible). They saw me and raised their mug in a salute, the salute of the Froststeppe Halls, even! Not only had I found a dwarf worthy of my time, but I had found a dwarf from my very own Hall. Repsed, of the Clan Ironset, of the proud and noble Hall Froststeppe. Have you ever met them, Cousin? I have met my share of the Clan and heard tales of their crafting skills, but never sat down to share a stein with one of the best damn smiths in any lands, in any halls.

Repsed is just like me, a good person being forced to put on dancing shoes and step around humans. The closer I got, the more I could smell the forge-sweat on their skin, the smoke woven into their dark hair, and it made me far more drunk that the mug of "ale" in front of me.

We bid the human servants to bring us food while we spoke and laughed of old times in the Halls. True diplomats, born and bred for such life, flitted around us like insects, while we supped on roast boar. When I kissed them and rubbed my own beard against that glorious mane of theirs, I could taste the meat on their breath. Beautiful.

A room in the inn was procured in no time, and we made it as similar to home as we could: snuffing the foolishly bright fires the humans put in every room, covering the windows and rediscovering the actual darkness. No longer blinded by the fires, I could gaze upon them, the thick bowing of a muscled chest and sturdy legs spread wide and bold, hidden beneath some of the best gear gold could buy. And Cousin, as much as I could have looked at the gear alone for hours, I wanted to see the body underneath. The humans brought up the last of our feastings and left us be, and I set about feeding my eyes and my hands as well as my belly.

Such breasts you have never seen. I would challenge you to find a dwarf anywhere, from any Hall, with as firm and full a bosom as Repsed. More than two handfuls on each side, with nipples black as coal and lush hair spanning every inch even after I had pushed aside their beard, thick and dark as a mountain forest. Two very curving mountains, that is. My own chest seemed meager and unripe in comparison, though they chuckled with delight at the sight of the bright red hair spread across my own. They had such firm hands: not quite the strength of a soldier's, but the steadiness of a true smith's.

They were soon laughing at my attempts to please those breasts, big full chortles that shook their frame and probably sent the humans outside scurrying like mice. My hands could only do so much on a firm chest like that. My mouth and beard could raise a flush on their dark skin and mix a groan or two into the laughter, however, so never let it be said that I have lost any deftness in my age.

Repsed pushed me onto one of the giant soft bricks of a bed and paid their own attention to my chest, all hard sucks and full twists over my nipples. They were hard enough to cut diamond by then, I tell you, Cousin. Or onyx, if I really wanted to cut into this mate!

The time for opening trifles had passed and we both shucked off our trousers and under-padding. Here was a great jest about removing my boots that I will have to relate in person when next I see you, as paper cannot hold the humor. I tell you truly, I felt like I was home, sharing a good joke with my fellows in the Hall.

The fur from their stomach plunged lower and thickened gloriously over their hips. I fumbled and felt through hair, looking for something, anything, to wrap my grip around! And just about cut myself on a clit as hard as a jagged piece of stone.

Repsed had an inner cave, and a mighty one at that; a person filled with their own hallowed hall. I confess myself briefly dismayed. I think a babe created by the two of us would be a fine and sturdy child, and had Repsed had a cock, I might have bargained to be filled up. But parting through that hair (and only getting lost once! Ha!), I could not have asked for anything more.

Thick and full lips in a large arc between their legs, with that perfect rigid clit seated like a jewel above. I took Repsed around the belly and flipped them down onto the bed, just so I could feast my eyes. You know I have strong hands, Cousin, worn and toughened from training and battle. But these fingers looked small and weak as an elf's when I slipped them across, against, and into that bold cunt. Over a hand-span across, more than a hand-length from clit to arse; Repsed could gestate their babes longer if they wanted and push out fully formed two-year-olds!

I started a proper exploration of their cave, and the warmth and strength surrounded my fingers. I hooked them inside, pulling up and rubbing against Repsed's bumps and contours and when I pushed hard against a certain treasure trove, they bellowed near loud enough to bring the inn down around our ears. Or maybe just their ears, as my ears were busy in their grip, with them trying to push my mouth towards their cunt. They could swallow me whole with that thing if they put their mind to it. But I can hold my own in a struggle and I was not about to be rushed. For their entire smithing prowess, muscles formed over a forge cannot beat those cut on an axe.

I pressed my fingers deeper in and near lost my nose when they bucked their hips up. A worthy way to receive an injury, but not one that would mesh well with a diplomatic mission; these humans can be so squeamish about a good and natural lay. A third and fourth finger fit in just as smoothly, but once I was in, that cave was not about to let me go: muscles all around me, giving a good proper squeeze to my hand and letting me feel a whole rush of blood and pulse. Firm and full and flush, just like the rest of them.

I mentioned this to Repsed while my hand was inside them, and they raised a tankard from the table in a toast. Then handed me another tankard so that we could properly commemorate the occasion. Rarely in my life has one perfect drink directly proceeded another.

The taste of them was amazing, Cousin. All fresh sweat and metallic tang across my tongue when I brushed past hair to lick over their folds. Their hands tangled in my hair and pushed me down against them, and the next thing I knew, I had heels digging into my back and thighs crushing my head. A proper way to please someone, I think, and a glorious reception into a cunt that deep. Hand inside, tongue busy out front, and neck surrounded by legs, I did my dwarven best by Repsed, up until the thrilling moment when they came so hard they nearly pulled my hair out while pushing me away. Let me tell you, my beard was plenty wet then.

With anyone less impressive than Repsed, my story might have ended there, or turned repetitive in the telling of them pleasing me with their tongue (which I would have relished, but it was not the way events would unfold). We spread out the remains of our feast on the tables and chairs of the room, replenishing our energy on the roast boar and laughing over some merriments. Our beards were tangled messes and I surely looked completely undone, even as I had been the one completing any doing. But over the third tankard of ale, our conversation turned to Repsed's recent work, and a bright glint took over their eyes.

They dug through their bag, tossing aside beautiful pieces of metalwork without a care, and pulled out the most amazing golden dildo I have ever seen in my life. Cousin, you would have wept to have seen the engravings, the curves and grooves, the secure seating for a harness, and the smooth polished opal that formed a bulbed head, perfectly placed to tease and please even the most experienced cunt. I reached out a hand and could wrap my entire fist around the shaft. Repsed laughed at my blatant awe. "You think it feels good in your hand? You've forgotten which parts it's for! You really have been gone from the Hall for too long!"

The dishes were set aside, the goblets rested on the floor, and my undergarments soon accompanied them as Repsed spread me on the bed before them, flush on my stomach.

A bottle of mineral oil soon followed the dildo out of the bag, and a harness of some of the finest treated leather; this was no bag of juvenile fumblings, but a true crafted arsenal. Their hand came down in a pert smack over my arse, and then down shifted to thumb apart my folds, already soaked with anticipation.

"Ah, you have a cave yourself!" they exclaimed. "I had wondered about asking for a babe. Not to be, I suppose." They laughed. I know I keep mentioning the laugh, but my ears felt drunk on the sound. I hope to carry it in my head, and feel it resonate in my loins, for many journeys ahead. They laughed and said, "I have a choice of holes now." They slapped my arse hard enough to rock me down onto the bed.

"Are you looking to bruise those holes as well?" I asked. Their hand dug into the stinging spot and drew my cheeks apart.

"Hush, you babe." They did pause, though. "If I do cause harm—"

"I know my limits. And I know to speak up when they're reached. Do you know to fuck when you're told?"

The cold metal teased through my hair and had me squirming. I have had my share of cocks: metal, stone, wood, those attached to others. But never have I been able to appreciate such craftsmanship with my lips alone. A squirt of the oil eased the slide into me and I groaned at the sheer width of the thing. I felt spread open, stretched and filled without being broken. I clenched down around the metal, squeezed when they drew it back and had me feeling each individual bump. The rock of their hips, a squirm here and there, and I was a howling mess impaled on a golden rod.

No sooner had I established a rhythm then they pulled the cock out and urged me onto my back. I groaned at even the least moment away from it, but the jewel glittered in the dim light, almost as bright as Repsed's leer when they took my breasts in hand. They squeezed and kneaded and twisted their fingers through my chest hair, with a tug and a push down just as the opal rubbed over my clit. I just about roared, Cousin, before they started pounding into me properly, angling the jewel up inside me and fucking me with the hard length. It was glorious, a tumble of hot breath and sweat and spit and oil and a bed we literally shook to bits at the frame. We thumped down the ridiculous distance to the floor, but Repsed's speed did not falter. In and out, an occasional retreat to rub the metal over my clit, then back to pounding.

I swear to you, when they twisted my breast with one hand, rubbed my clit with the other and rocked hard against my hips, and I came with the force of a sledgehammer. One giant, throbbing tension, then a mighty release that left every muscle and sinew slack on my bones. It took all the energy in me just to find the will to keep breathing.

Repsed beamed at the spent dwarf before them and the flood of wetness between us. A brief moment to tend to their tools, as all good craftspeople do, and they tumbled down onto the broken bed beside me. Once more I tell you, with the greatest sincerity I can muster, that it was the finest fuck I have ever had.

The morning came, as it must when you spend your time above ground. We devoured the rest of the cold meat and bread, and enjoyed more of the human food for breakfast (although why humans view bird egg as an acceptable food, I will never understand). We divided the costs of the damages to the inn, as all diplomats ultimately must, and bid our farewells.

I know where Repsed's travels will take them and where letters may find them; I hope that they and I may meet again in this lifetime. Even if no return to a shared bed could yield similar results, I would rejoice to share a drink and a meal with such a proud and jovial dwarf. But I would certainly not say no to another ride on that golden cock.

Cousin, as it may be some time yet before I return to the Hall, I ask you to please send a barrel of our Clan's best beer to the Clan Ironset, in honor and recognition of the night I have spent with one of their numbers. Any Clan should be proud to have such an efficient and effective sex-smith among their lineage, and I shall visit them personally to bestow my respects when I next return home. A time which cannot come quickly enough, in my reckoning. Repsed has made me long even more for the company of dwarves, even as they are a breed apart from the rest of us.

Thank you for your attentions, Cousin. I would be thrilled to hear of your exploits in the Hall, to live through you until I may return.

Yours truly and boldly, full of pride in the dwarven people and longing to return home once more,

THENDEN
  Of the Clan Stoneforest
  Of the Hall Froststeppe

To Those Who Move Mountains

by Jason Carpenter

BARIN LOOKED OVER AT Triff with a half grunt, half sigh. These mountains had been mined for generations by Barin's clan. The tunnels ran deep and seamless through the trove of treasures that nature itself had laid there. With hand, hook, and axe, Barin and his people made this range of mountains their own.

But the world was changing.

Sky ships cast long, slow shadows across the forest, while the boats that once traversed the rivers quietly now expelled white clouds of steam. Words like "machinery" and "gears" began to filter into the Dwarvish lexicon, and these words always seemed like more of ancient curses to Barin than the beneficial wonders that they were intended to be.

And now, Triff and his bag of tricks was here with Barin. The mountains, the last respite of Barin's clan, had been invaded by the outside world.

"Barin, Barin, hold up. You're going too fast," Triff exclaimed. Barin held up his lantern and turned to face the small-framed but still stocky dwarf known as Triff. In the deep and dark recesses of the caves, Barin was amazed to find his traveling companion still surprisingly clean. Barin's long black beard was matted cobwebs and dust, and his fingernails were blacker than a dead crow's claw. Triff's beard seemed to resist the dirt and grime like some enchantment. Dwarves were never ones for cleanliness, but for some reason the clean complexion of his companion forced Barin to look at the male dwarf in a more endearing light.

"Thank you for stopping," Triff said as he pulled a small package out of his sizeable shoulder pack and pressed it against the wall. It began to slide off before he pressed it again, then again once more until he was sure it would stay. Triff, satisfied with his work, began to unspool a long wire from another of his many other knapsacks he carried.

Barin snorted, not caring if he hid his resentment for Triff's current task at hand. "If you think that... whatever that is, magic clay can mine a mountain—"

"It's not clay..." Triff began.

"—when it can't even stay stuck on that tunnel wall, you're crazier that I thought you were. You, and others like you leave our people to be corrupted by the Elfish philosophers, and the schools of Man. And then, you come back here when you finally realize that they don't want you. That to them, you are nothing but a lesser!" Barin wanted to bite his tongue at those final words but remained stoic. Regardless of who Triff was, today he was here with his people. Where he belonged.

Triff patted the package one last time and looked toward Barin. Barin was the prototypical dwarf; broad shoulder, barrel chested, stocky and proud. With one hand he held the lantern up, with the other he gripped a massive war hammer. He needed no pack of supplies, no tricks or training. To Barin, the mountain was but a sand castle and he was the sea. Triff admired that.

"First off, you're right. I was corrupted by the teachings of others. Wide eyed at a world and a future beyond these caves. But you know why I came back? It's because I saw a world moving past manual labor into one of mechanized labor. Our entire lifeblood is based on being the ones who carve out the mountain ranges in search of treasure. But this," Triff said as he pointed to the knapsack on his arm, "this simple explosive can do the work of a hundred of us, and the crystals and gems we need are buried, are so powerful that they won't be scratched. So we need to get it to work before the Elves, before the Kingdoms, before anyone else. Because if one elf can do the work of our entire culture, then what do we have left?"

"Our honor," Barin boasted.

Triff shook his head. "Well, for now you are meant to be my guide through these tunnels. Let's just place the rest of these and call it a day. Tomorrow we can...."

In that moment, Triff noticed something he had never seen on another dwarf's face. He only recognized it because he had seen it many times on the faces of other species.

It was a look of fear. Just for a second, a split second before Barin regained his senses but it was long enough for Triff to feel his spine go cold.

"What...."

Barin held up his war hammer to silence Triff. He then motioned with it towards himself. 'Come here,' he mouthed silently in the torchlight. Triff felt his legs betray him. The light seemed to be growing dimmer as he moved slowly towards it. He could see Barin's face become tight with impatience.

And then Triff realized what was causing Barin so much anxiety.

Barin had smelt it first. His nose, even though it was packed tightly with mildew, would never forget that smell. He was a child the first time he encountered a RageWorm. It was over a century ago and many mountains over, but it had always haunted his mead-drenched dreams. The smell of earthen rot. The sound of click-clacking insectoid arms tattering against the cavern walls in the darkness. They were rare, sure, but no mountain was ever truly safe from them.

Triff suddenly felt a surge of adrenaline as he felt the Worm's warm breath coming down the tunnel behind him. He ran past Barin in the opposite direction. Barin quickly followed him.

"Which way do we..." Triff started before Barin answered him by pushing him down one side tunnel, then another. A deafening roar echoed through cavern system. The RageWorm was all spinning teeth and muscle mass as it chewed its own way through the mountain. It lived off minerals; dwarves just sometimes got in the way.

The RageWorm smashed down just feet in front of Barin and Triff. Rocks peppered them, nearly blinding them, but they both got a glimpse of one section of the mile-long monster as it made quick work of the millennium-old cavern system. Barin holstered his war hammer, even its massive weight but a child's toy against the Worm, and yanked Triff backwards. Barin began dragging him through the tunnels at random.

"I need my map," Triff protested. "We'll get lost!"

"Better than getting eaten," Barin replied as he continued to pull Triff this way and that. The Worm continued to devour its way around them and despite a few more close calls, Barin and Triff soon found themselves deeper inside the mountain than they had intended.

The raging sound of the Worm had been replaced with a quiet sound of an underground mountain river. Barin held the lantern aloft. White crystals sparkled all around them. The cave ceiling glimmered like stars at night.

"They're beautiful," Triff said.

"And worthless," Barin grunted, before adding almost apologetically, "but yes, they are beautiful nonetheless."

Barin and Triff unslung their gear and sat down on the river bank. Barin took off his boots and slipped his feet in the surprisingly warm water. Blind Nipsim fish swam across and tickled the skin of his large, brutish feet.

"So what happens now?"

Barin contemplated Triff's question for a moment. "Well," he began, "normally in a situation like this, we'd wait in a safe spot, like this, and when another digger team realized we were missing they'd rescue us. But that normally takes a week. Or more. But...." Barin motioned towards Triff's satchel of explosives.

Triff understood the implication. He may have been the architect of this plan, but when it came to putting it into motion, Triff and Barin were just one team among many. Triff remembered his proposal to the Dwarven High Council. A new way to mine mountains by cracking it open. "Why build a thousand tunnels when you can build just one, then line it with these powder packs and split the mountain in two?" The Council agreed on the plan, more out of curiosity than anything else. But there was one caveat: "The test will take place before sunrise on Elks Day," the Dwarven King Janamill said. "We can't have mining operations disrupted too long to play with your devices."

"But what if it's not ready? What if some of my team is stuck in the mountain? You can't mean to detonate while..." Triff protested.

"Dwarves die," the king answered solemnly. "We all give our lives for the mountain."

Barin's voice snapped Triff back to the present. "If it's any consolation, Triff, if this works you'll be a legend. And if it doesn't, well, you won't be around to be shamed out of the kingdom."

"Thanks," Triff said with a laugh. "I guess that's worth something."

Barin began to remove the rest of his armor. He set the worn yet sturdy mining gear on the river bank and then began to remove his leather under-armor.

"You seem quite calm for someone who's going to be crushed to death in a few hours," Triff said.

"Eh, it's not the first time I've been lost. Not even the first time I thought it was the end. Getting eaten by a RageWorm is one thing, but in times like this, where you just have to sit and wait, you have to learn not to take the last moments of your life so seriously." Barin undid the last ties of his leather and let them drop to the ground. His squat body was pure muscle. His calved were as hard as boulders and his chest stood out proud and chiseled. Barin's bare arms rippled with the muscles of a manual laborer. Without looking to see Triff's reaction to his nakedness, Barin slipped all the way into the warm darkness of the slow-moving underground river. Triff was alone for just a second as the lamp light flickered across the cavern walls.

Barin reemerged from the river. The water beaded across his forehead and soaked his great beard. He began shaking his head and let the water splash from his hair in all directions.

"I'm sure you've heard the rumors," Barin said to Triff.

"I... have," Triff replied. "They say that miners... when they're lost they get a little...."

"When forty miners get trapped, twenty couples get rescued," Barin laughed. Triff blushed. "Oh come now, my little worldly friend. You travel through the kingdoms of all the races and yet you blush like a child at the suggestion. Are you telling me you've never...."

"No," Triff answered quietly.

Barin backed off for a moment. Then he continued. "Triff, we can sit down here until someone up there decides to bring this mountain down, assuming that does work, twiddling our thumbs, or we can do what dwarves do. Have fun, and celebrate life, celebrate our lives, even in the end we are dwarves. We may have no mead or smoke, but we do have each other."

Triff looked around, almost as if checking if they truly were alone. Then he turned back to Barin.

"Well," Triff said, "We do have some mead." Barin laughed as Triff reached into one of his satchels and pulled out a sealed jar.

"Come join me, Triff. We will celebrate your plan in our own way."

Triff stood up. He slowly began to remove his armor. It was less substantial than Barin's but required to do the job. He felt Barin's eyes on him as he began to undo his leathers. Triff *had* heard the stories of bawdy miners having their way with each other deep in the mountains. He had always laughed about them but was also fascinated at the same time. Surely, he would not be one to be with another male dwarf. But why not? If the manliest of them could do it with a laugh, why was it so alien to him? Triff, ever the scholar, decided to make the most of this opportunity. He locked his eyes with Barin as he slowly stepped out of his leather under-armor. He saw a smile flicker on Barin's face. He liked what he saw.

Triff was still as stocky as any dwarf but his muscles were leaner. His beard was neatly trimmed and hung down just past his neck. Where Barin's chest seemed to be covered in hair, Triff's chest was covered with a lighter tuft. But Triff soon noticed that Barin wasn't looking at his beard or his chest.

Triff's thick cock was half-erect. It surprised him to feel the blood rushing so quickly to his dwarfhood. Barin beckoned to Triff. Triff picked up the jar of mead and made his way, a little slowly and more suggestive than Triff would have thought he was capable of, to the edge of the river.

Barin reached up out of the water and began to run his warm, wet hands across Triff's naked legs. Triff sat down and let his legs dangle into the river.

"So do you want a drink or," Triff started before he felt Barin's mouth envelop his now very hard cock. Triff watched the beefy dwarf's head bob up and down. If he had still been standing Triff would have no doubt felt his knees buckle but now he just felt his toes curl as lips and tongue slid across his meaty shaft.

The cavern river seemed to bubble like a brook in the near darkness. The sound of unseen fish splashing could also be heard. But Triff could only hear the sounds of his own slight moans echoing through the emptiness.

Barin slipped the slick cock out of his mouth. "Isn't this a better way to pass the time?"

"I thought you hated me."

Barin laughed. "I do." He flicked his tongue across the tip of Triff's thick head. "I do, but that just makes this all a lot more fun."

It took a second for Triff to realize what he meant, but as Barin began to teasingly lick Triff's shaft he caught on. Barin was going to torment him as long as he could.

Reaching for the jar of mead, Triff opened it up and took a big swig. Barin continued to play with Triff's thick and succulent dick. Triff leaned back on one arm and with the free hand took another drink of the mead.

Barin began to move his mouth rhythmically up and down on Triff's cock. Triff began moaning again, and Barin's muffled moans could also be heard as he slurped and sucked. Triff felt his balance leaving him and he sat the jar down before he dropped it. Reason and logic were leaving his head now. The thoughts of being lost down here forever seemed to disappear as Barin's expert tongue worked its way around his shaft. Now he knew why the miners did this. Comfort in each other, even in the most desperate of situations....

Triff's thought process stopped completely. He felt a surge rise up from deep inside him. Barin was now sucking furiously and each slurp was loud, a near-gagging noise. Triff grabbed two handfuls of Barin's thick hair and began riding his face. The passion had taken him completely over now. Never before had he felt so right, so part of someone. He began thrusting up as Barin suckled down. The rhythm was perfect and then he felt it all rush out of him.

Wave after wave of pleasure racked his body. Triff's balls emptied into Barin's warm and wanting mouth, and Barin greedily swallowed it all. Even as Triff was coming, Barin continued to run his lips up and down his shaft, causing Triff to shiver with pleasure even more. Eventually the last long stream of come shot out of Triff's cock, and he collapsed backwards.

The silence of the cave was broken by the sound of Barin's heavy breathing and Triff's near-hysterical laughter.

"That was, oh, that was amazing, I mean, wow, I can't think of anything, oh my, I'm just so, wow," Triff said in between laughs. His eyes seemed unable to focus on any one thing in the room. His bare back was cold on the cavern floor, but he could be lying on a bed of nails and he wouldn't have noticed. His entire body tingled.

Barin began to slowly move out of the dark water. He spread Triff's legs open and pulled him towards him. Triff was still laughing before he realized what was happening.

Triff looked between his own legs, past his tired cock, to see Barin's own beefy and massive cock barreling down towards his waist. Triff stared long and hard at the hard and long dwarf meat coming towards him, and despite his exhaustion just a few moments earlier, he felt his dick begin to shudder to life once more.

Barin pulled Triff even closer. Triff felt the mass of Barin's unleashed bulge press against his tight ass cheeks. Barin placed his large, rough hands around Triff's waist. They locked eyes for a moment. Triff was still semi-delirious, but he could see the lust and wanton desire burning in Barin's eyes.

"Let me put a little girth in your Middle-Earth," Barin said. Triff laughed out loud at the storybook pun before he realized that what Barin was putting in him was anything but little. Barin's cock seemed to split Triff in two. If it was not for the lubrication of the river water, Triff was sure he would have been irrevocably broken. But the discomfort seemed to pass as Barin found his way deeper and deeper inside Triff. Triff leaned back and breathed in deeply with each small thrust. He felt Barin was being as gentle as he could with such a large member.

As Barin continued to penetrate Triff, Triff felt his mind begin to collapse. The pleasure and the pressure of something so large and alive inside his own body made his pulse pound. Each second it seemed to grow larger and become part of him. It inched its way deeper and wider. Triff's eyes rolled back once again in pleasure as he took another deep breath. And just when he didn't think he could handle any more he heard Barin say: "Just a little deeper. I'm almost there."

Triff felt his cock go fully erect. This monster of a dwarf was a real male. A thick, hung, dirty, strong, abrasive dwarf warrior that the kingdom had sung songs about for generations. And he was deep inside Triff, making him a part of Barin. Triff felt Barin's cock throb so deep inside of him. He wrapped his legs around Barin's waist and pulled him in all the way, gasping as he felt Barin's balls slap against his tight ass.

Barin stood there for a moment as he felt Triff's tight ass adjust to his cock. Then, slowly reaching behind him, he unhooked Triff's ankles from his waist and spread Triff's legs wide into the air. Triff shuddered with unrestrained pleasure at the thought of being so vulnerable. Without another word Barin slowly slid his cock halfway out of Triff before sliding it back inside.

Triff felt everything. Each long, slow thrust made his entire body vibrate. Nothing seemed clear in his head. He bit his lip and closed his eyes. He couldn't tell if Barin was thrusting into him, or if Barin was pulling Triff onto his cock, or both, it didn't matter. His mind was soup. The thick meat moved in and out of him like a piston at the fire forges.

Barin began grunting. The thrusts became deeper and faster. Triff's entire body collapsed onto one single point deep inside of his body like a black hole. Nothing seemed to matter but that tight bundle of nerves that Barin kept pounding over and over and over again. Triff was helpless to stop Barin even if he had wanted to. Barin kept a firm hold on Triff's ankles, holding them up high and spreading him wide. Barin's long beard rubbed across Triff's naked stomach. The burly dwarf continued to pump himself into Triff's virgin asshole.

"Don't stop," Triff moaned.

"Wasn't planning on it," Barin said with a grunt as he pushed balls-deep back into Triff. "Bet now you wish you spent more time in the mines than with your books, huh?"

"Oh don't stop, keep fucking me,"

"I asked you a question, city dwarf," Barin replied.

Triff's body was racked with waves of ecstasy. "Oh, ugh yeah, make me yours, fuck, fuck me harder."

Barin laughed out loud but never stopped pounding inside of Triff. The slapping sound of dwarf on dwarf reverberated through the cavern system.

Triff's cock was as hard as Barin's now. It stuck up like a monument to passion and bounced back and forth with each thrust. His cock began to get slick with sweat and precome. Triff couldn't take it anymore.

Triff began to rotate his ass back and forth, side to side, grinding against Barin's thrusts. He felt it deep inside of him. Barin's cock head pushing up against his prostate. Triff continued to grind as his moans grew louder and longer.

Barin's own cockiness began to fade as he too was swept up in the moment. The deep thrusts become more focused and faster and played against each of Triff's grinding movements. Barin looked down at the dwarf laying beneath him, splayed out and groaning from the pleasure he was giving Triff. Barin felt his own balls begin to tighten as the inevitable came.

Triff felt Barin explode inside of him. Warmth blasted into his already hot hole, but he felt every wet drop splash inside of him. His own cock exploded just seconds later, and he covered his own stomach and most of Barin's beard with his milky come. Barin continued to thrust as Triff's body spasmed. Groans became grunts as each thrust resulted in another stream of juice inside of Triff.

Barin reluctantly slipped his cock out of Triff, and Triff felt oddly empty. Barin rolled onto his back and lay next to Triff's panting body. Barin took in a deep breath and smelled the cold air of the cave.

"So do you really think this plan is going to work?" Barin asked.

"Huh, what?" was Triff's only reply. Barin laughed his deep laugh again.

"Your brain is fried, Triff. Get some sleep. I'll see if I can find a way out."

"Can we... you know, if you can't can we...."

"Get some sleep," Barin repeated. Triff closed his tired eyes as his worn body fell limp.

BA-DOOM. The sound echoed through the air, jolting Triff awake. His eyes opened not to the darkness of the cave but to bright sunlight carving beams through forest branches. He knew he was moving but not walking because he felt the leaves smash against his face but his feet didn't touch the ground.

BA-DOOM BA-DOOM. Two more explosions rocked the mountain range. Triff suddenly realized he was outside and Barin was carrying him. He also realized they were startlingly close to the mountain as the explosives continued to detonate.

"We're free?" Triff asked groggily.

"How much mead did you drink?" Barin grunted as he continued to run with Triff's body slung over his shoulder. "I've been trying to wake you for hours!"

"Barin! Barin, stop! Look!"

Barin swung around towards the mountain range. He stood in stunned silence. Triff slid his naked body down and stood next to Barin.

A ring of explosions ripped through the mountain. Two rows. Then three. Although Barin and Triff were too close for comfort, the view was also too good to miss. Thousands of tons of worthless rocks, and one dead RageWorm, fell down the mountainside in chunks. And even from their vantage point deep in the valley they could see what was left in key sections of the mountain appeared to be, no, it was, the precious gems and minerals that would keep the Dwarf kingdoms powerful for generations.

"The technology only makes the job easier," Triff said. "Not obsolete."

Barin considered this for a moment. He had lost many friends over the decades to the perils of mining.

"Maybe there is honor in using the technology of the other nations to make ours even greater. And safer."

"And there is always honor in being a rich dwarf," Triff added.

Triff and Barin began marching through the underbrush back towards the mountain. Soon they would meet up with the other teams and celebrate their success. And later that night, Triff and Barin would celebrate on their own.

Don't Screw the Messenger

by Jessica McHugh

HE COLLAPSES AGAINST the door with a groan. "How did I get myself into this?"

"Desperation" is the only answer. An orphan boy born into royal service, Balthasar has spent the majority of his eighteen years working as a messenger in the kingdom of Auralom. He'd started wondering ages ago if he'd ever see other lands, fearing the longer they went unseen, the more they'd fade from existence. It was terrifying enough a prospect that he prepared himself to do anything for freedom, including the fool's errand that brings him to yet another stranger's door.

After nearly a month of cataloging names for the queen, Balthasar's body is bent—not from exhaustion, but from loneliness. His back and legs ache from the weight of isolation, which hunkers down on his shoulders like his own personal ogre. It throttles his head and mocks him each time he's forced to move on after collecting a beautiful woman's name. For despite the many ladies he's encountered on this journey, it seems ages since he's been touched. While the ogre of loneliness beats nearly every inch of the messenger's arms and legs black and blue, another appendage aches from neglect.

Balthasar can't muster the energy to knock. His eyes flutter closed as he leans his cheek against the door and exhales a gust of sorrow. When they open again, he stares into the gaze of a younger boy standing in the nearby window. He smiles and offers a tiny wave, but the boy doesn't reciprocate. He instead screams for his mother, whose scowling face promptly appears behind the glass. Balthasar backpedals in shock, faster after he watches her pluck a gun from the wall. The door flies open with a draft nearly as cold as the gun barrel the woman plants against his forehead.

"What are you doing out here, boy?"

Balthasar holds up his royal seal, and her matronly rigor disappears. She shushes the dog howling in the house and sets down the gun.

"I need names," he says hurriedly. "Your name. Your son's name. You might as well give me the dog's name too."

"What's this all about? Have we done something wrong?"

"Please, Misses—"

She chirps, "Miss" and steps aside to welcome him inside.

He enters, sighing as he inhales the robust warmth of stew bubbling over her hearth. Facing the woman, he straightens his back, his bones cracking more than his age should allow, and holds up his list.

"Miss, I am an official messenger of Her Most Royal Majesty, and I have more houses to visit before this night is through. If you would give me your names, I'll be on my way."

"My name is Halencia, and my son's name is Joval. The dog is Tom," she answers.

"The dog is Tom?"

"Yes. Tom," she says flatly as Balthasar jots the names on his pad. "What is this for anyway?"

"I'm afraid I can't say, Miss, but I thank you for your time." He bows and heads for the door.

"You never told me your name, messenger."

"It's Balthasar."

He twists the doorknob, but the woman halts him, first curling her fingers over his shoulder, then draping her body against his back.

"Go to bed, Joval, and take Tom with you," she says, pressing her breasts so deliberately to Balthasar's body he feels her heart beat rapidly against his spine.

He's about to contest the closeness when she breathes "Balthasar" into his ear, and his fatigue gives way to something else. How her fingertips hook into his flesh, how she firmly stamps the back of his neck with kisses, it reminds him of the last woman he had—or the woman that had *him*, more appropriately.

While Queen Moira of Auralom had converted several servants into lovers, she frequently professed her favoritism to Balthasar. Although they'd never had intercourse, he possessed such an outstanding talent with his tongue that the queen agreed to liberate him from royal service if he could satisfy her orally without waking the king. Driven by his desire for freedom, he'd agreed to the terms, believing wholeheartedly the queen would honor them. It was the greatest mistake of his life.

He still feels the burn of the whip that night. After pleasuring the queen, after cuckolding her slumbering husband, after setting off to seek a better future beyond the castle gates, Balthasar found himself mired in a deeper plot. He hadn't laid one foot upon free soil before the royal guards detained and charged him with assault against Her Most Gracious Majesty. Moira granted him clemency so he only received a whipping, but the brutality left him changed forever. As he lay bleeding in the dungeon, Balthasar prayed for a different kind of freedom. But he didn't die that evening, and the scars of his naivety have since served as a painful reminder of his lowly station.

Once the young boy and dog disappear upstairs, Halencia spins Balthasar to face her and flings open his vest. As her hands claw his chest and skate down his back, his skin prickles with sweaty longing. He wonders if she feels the scars through his tunic, or whether she'd be less romantically inclined if she saw the twisted tracks of flesh. His mind dips into a fantasy of her tongue tracing his bad memories, but when she tries easing the list of names from his hand, he snaps back to reality.

"I'm afraid I must decline," he says, exhaling a steadying breath. "I have a long night ahead of me."

Halencia kisses his neck hungrily. "You certainly do."

Balthasar gulps through his growing desire. "And this one is the most important night of all. It's the full moon."

"Is that so?" she murmurs, her lips moving down his chest. Discovering the dagger at his waist, she chuckles. "Your blade looks as sharp as its first day out of the shop. How many times have you used it?"

"Never."

She bites her lip. "Would you?"

"If it were necessary."

"You don't worry what comes after killing? The guilt might be with you forever, boy."

"What makes you think I would feel guilty?" he asks. "Besides, after a kill or two, maybe people wouldn't call me 'boy' anymore."

"You don't need to kill to be a man," Halencia says. She runs her tongue up his throat and sucks on his bottom lip.

He gives in for a moment, his lust rising as he savors her juicy kiss, but he remembers the list again. As his only remaining hope for departure, it must be completed and delivered to Queen Moira before the full moon hit its peak. The details of the task weren't fully revealed—only that the messenger would need to spend a month circulating the kingdom collecting names, or the king and queen's newborn son would die. Why, Balthasar didn't care. He only thought of the reward the king had promised: he who delivered the "right name" would be granted his greatest wish.

Musings of sweet freedom swirl through Balthasar's mind as he whispers, "I have to go. I have to find more names."

Halencia smirks and snaps open his braces. "What's in a name?"

"I don't know, but a lot rests on this one—my god, your hair smells like dandelions—and it has something to do with the queen and her new child."

Halencia backs off with her brow furrowed. After a few seconds, she smacks her forehead and laughs.

"A dwarf pact," she says.

"What?"

"How does a miller's daughter become a queen overnight? How does she spin straw into gold? I should've known a dwarf had his hand in it. Little buggers like to have their hands in everything, trust me."

"Can't say I know much about dwarves."

"Well, I do. I needed a name once, too, but I failed." She clamps her hands to Balthasar's shoulders and grins. "You won't fail, Balthasar. I can help you, and get some payback of my own."

"Payback for what?"

"I used to have a husband. Now I have a dog named Tom. Enough said?" She traces his face with her fingertips and dances them over his lips. "And if I do help you, what will you give me in return?"

"I have nothing to give. If I succeed, I will leave Auralom. More than anything, I want to explore new worlds."

Her hand moves down his chest, over his stomach, and clamps onto the hardening bulge between his legs. "I can show you new worlds, and you needn't leave Auralom to enter them."

Squeezing his manhood, Halencia pulls Balthasar to her lips. Her kiss pries his mouth open, and she fills it with her hot tongue, tasting of cinnamon bread. His groin aches against her palm, sending delicious shivers throughout his body. When the kiss breaks, his eyes remain closed, his head lolling on his shoulders.

"I can help you, Balthasar. We can help each other," she whispers. "I've been so lonely."

In a blink, lust transforms from an idea into a palpable thing. All the worlds he'd longed to see mean nothing once she clamps his hand between her legs. There's such warmth, such wonder there. He could be an explorer yet.

Halencia pushes her undergarments aside and guides his fingers inside her. "Stay with me," she says. "Stay forever."

Nothing beside remains when "forever" drips hot lust onto his palm. The word minimizes with her moans, as if her pleasure in rocking against his hand swallows all vocabulary. When she liberates his erection, his lifelong dream is just language crushed beneath her passion, mere pumps from disappearing into her for all time.

A dog barks, and reality reappears. Balthasar grits his teeth as he backs away, buttoning his pants.

"I can't do this now," he says. "I'm sorry, but I need to complete my task."

Balthasar kisses her hand as he bows, then marches for the door. But Halencia chases after, throwing her body between him and the exit. She gathers his collar in her fists and plants her cheek against his. Sucking on his earlobe, she whispers. "You have hours yet before the full moon rises. Spend them in my arms."

Halencia gazes deep into his eyes, and smiles. Her lips part, and when she exhales a thin breath that smells of flowers, Balthasar's vision blurs, and his eyelids droop. He nods dreamily as his gaze spins around the house. Pots and pans gleam from the kitchen, the fire reflected in the metal, but the shapes twist and stretch into stone pillars and ledges.

"You don't look so good, darling," she whispers. "I don't think you should go anywhere."

She pushes Balthasar onto a shelf and, straddling his lap, places his hands on her breasts. Balthasar groans as Halencia grinds him into the stone, his mind emptying with each pleasurable swell. All he knows is the ecstasy in finally conquering his loneliness.

A cackle from the kitchen draws his attention. Peering over Halencia's shoulder, Balthasar spots the shadow of a small, stout man. The figure's arm pumps back and forth. Another shadow appears behind a chair, and another by the bathroom. He soon sees theme everywhere, and no longer obscured. The stunted men crouched in the dark of Halencia's cottage beat their cocks, harder when the lady of the house frees her breasts. Some rub their bare chests or stroke their beards. Others suck on their fingers and grunt through their pleasure, culminating in a communal ejaculation that causes each dwarf to flicker like a flame.

Balthasar jumps to his feet, knocking Halencia to the floor as he runs to the door. Ripping it open, he dashes outside and collapses on her doorstep, brow dappled with sweat. As he stands, he still feels Halencia's tongue entwined with his, like a phantom limb he desperately needs to survive, and his cock throbs in protest as he starts away from her house. Halencia's dog leaps into Balthsar's path before he can cross out of the yard. He tries to sidestep it, but the mutt slaps its paws on top of the messenger's feet.

"What's the big idea, Rover?"

The dog digs at the ground before rearing up on two legs. It glimmers in the setting sun, the name "Tom" illuminated in gold. The dog emits a low howl and gallops in a circle.

"I can't play now, boy. I have work to do."

He shuffles around the dog to leave, but Tom scuttles up behind Balthasar and nips his ass. Screeching, he leaps three feet in the air. While he rubs the sore spot, Tom the dog yips and runs to a nearby oak tree. Dusk has fallen and he needs to pick up speed, but when the dog appears to nod, even beckon Balthasar with his head, he jogs over to the massive tree.

It looks normal enough, but it feels to Balthasar like penetrating an invisible, viscous wall as he passes under the leaves. His mind feels sharper in the shade, and his energy increases, but the strangest difference becomes obvious when Tom the dog says, "You're in grave danger, boy."

Balthasar gasps. "You can talk? Does that mean you were human? And married to Halencia?"

His head is bowed so low his snout skirts the ground. "Yes. I suppose we're technically still married, but she doesn't exactly give me a husband's respect anymore."

"Does she know you can talk?"

"No, and I beg you to keep your voice down so she won't find out," he says. "This tree is a weak spot in the magic spell protecting her house. It's the only place that still exposes a sliver of my true form, and the true form of the dwarves who weaved the magic."

"Why would she let them do that? She hates dwarves."

Tom's lip curls, and his massive fangs glint as he says, "Does she? Take my advice, boy, you'd do better listening to this mutt over that bitch. Go to that window, and tell me what you see."

Balthasar huffs as he stomps out from under the tree and ducks under Halencia's kitchen window. Peeking in, he watches as she licks pink frosting from her fingers and resumes decorating her cake. With her back to him, she grates chocolate into a bowl, humming a jaunty tune as the young boy dances behind her.

Balthasar returns to the tree, shaking his head. "She's baking a cake. What's so sinister about that?"

Tom wheezes a chuckle and says, "Now look from where you're standing now."

Peering through the dusk, Balthasar sees the house's interior changed. Instead of the kitchen, Halencia now stands in a cave, surrounded by ledges and pillars of rock glittering with gems. Halencia's back is still to him, but her clothes are gone, and her hums have changed to moans. The young boy's hair has changed to a gray mess of curls that match his beard, only slightly visible behind his ears while the dwarf's face is buried in Halencia's pussy. Her engorged lips glisten when he pauses to wipe his chin. Then, grasping her ass, he shoves three fingers inside her, making her hump backwards, grunting in gratitude as her come splashes across his face.

But the gray-haired dwarf isn't the only one to enjoy her. When she rears back, he realizes a chubby dwarf stands on the counter in front of her, his swollen cock wet with her saliva. A red-bearded man pushes a stepstool behind her and looses his member while the gray-haired dwarf crouches beneath her and sucks on her clit. Dozens of dwarfs encircle them, stroking their cocks as they wait for their turn and dance to the jovial music played by the wild-whiskered fiddler.

They leap from foot to foot as they sing along, occasionally spilling ale on their masturbating brethren, but no one seems to mind the shower. While a few lick themselves clean and waggle their tongues for more ale, others use the spillage as lubrication. Only a few dwarves have bulbous bald heads gleaming in the sunset, but every man sports a beard, whether cropped or hanging so low it adds a few stumbles into their dances.

Balthasar's heart pounds, and his erection threatens to bust open his britches. Covering his crotch, he kneels beside Tom the dog.

"What are they doing to her?"

"Exactly what she wants," he says.

"But they weren't there a minute ago."

"Dwarves don't want to be found, Balthasar. Each group has its own tricks to stay hidden. This one cast a charm that hides the truth from passersby and visitors." When a new cacophonous melody rings from the fiddler, the dog whispers, "Ah, here we go. These fools are always bragging about tricking humans. Just listen, and I believe you'll find the name you need."

When Halencia comes again, her lovers switch places. Two mouths latch onto her breasts, suckling as she fills her own mouth with the colossal cock of a bald dwarf. The fellow climaxes almost immediately, and pearly cream drips down her chin. She licks it from her face and swallows hard as she crawls onto a ledge and positions herself on all fours.

As new dwarves go to work on her, others raise their goblets in celebration, and the fiddler raises his voice in song.

> *In the spring, when hearts are often flighty,*
> *Paerdarn was summoned by a hero mighty.*
> *He wanted a woman clad in lace*

To sit and grind on his rugged face.
So Paerdarn granted the hero's beg
And delivered a girl who'd spread her legs.
"But on the next full moon," Paerdarn said,
"You must pass my test to keep your head.
Guess my name, and she's ever yours:
To eat in bed, on couch, and floor."
But the soldier lost both test and dame
When he couldn't guess Paerdarn's name.

A fisherman asked for a cock so big
Every woman in town would flip her wig.
He called Bahasta, who appeared and sang,
"I can give you the world's most awesome wang.
But when the next full moon arrives,
You must guess my name to keep your size."
The fisherman laughed as his member grew,
Ignoring the task he'd have to do.
He had no answer by the next full moon,
And his cock shriveled to a rotten prune.
Now he hides away his tiny shame.
Because he couldn't guess Bahasta's name.

A girl wanted her man to bring her silk,
Instead of things like bread and milk.
She said, "I'm a lovely, modern wife,
And I need a much more lavish life.
I'm living in a house like a pungent bog,
And my husband's no better than a dog."
So she called Golashin to change her man
Into a husband who made her grand.
But the bitch's riches didn't last,
And her husband's shape shifted fast.

Another full moon changed the game
Because she didn't guess Golashin's name

"You?" Balthasar asks, and Tom nods. "Why did he punish you instead of her?"

With his snout pointed at the kitchen, he whines. "She made a better deal."

Halencia howls as two dwarves penetrate her from behind, the small of her back shiny with ejaculate.

> *Ladies of all kinds crave a taste*
> *Of another man from another race.*
> *A dwarven cock is hard as stone,*
> *To make them shimmy, scream, and moan.*
> *Even within our bedeviled pact*
> *None resist our wiles. (That's a fact!)*
> *After helping her spin straw to gold,*
> *I helped my lady smoke my pole.*
> *I fucked her once, and from our fun,*
> *She conceived my blessed dwarven son.*
> *Soon my progeny I'll go to claim,*
> *For she won't guess Rumpelstiltskin is my name!*

Balthasar shouts "Rumpelstiltskin!" in excitement, which switches to fear when dozens of eyes snap to the window. He assumes there are a few dozen he can't see below the window as well.

Tom barks, "You dolt!" and dashes away from the messenger boy.

The fiddler stands on the rocky windowsill, his lengthy beard thrown over his shoulder. His long, thin nose presses against the pane, and when he parts his lips, the gate of ivory pebbles he calls teeth remain clenched.

Balthasar tries to dash away, but when Rumpelstiltskin reaches out, clenching his fist, the ground rumbles. Columns of rock rise from the earth, surrounding and entrapping Balthasar beneath the tree.

Tilting his head, Rumpelstiltskin hisses. "It's that messenger. I thought we told you to get rid of him, Halencia."

"I tried, I swear!"

"Never mind that now," he says. "What did you hear, boy?"

Balthasar crumples against his stone cage. "Everything. I know your name. I know you're going to steal the queen's child. And I suppose I know you'll kill me now, won't you?"

Rumpelstiltskin laughs. "Why would I do that? There are no rules in my bargain forbidding investigation. You discovered my name fair and square. By all means, take it back to your kingdom."

He unclenches his fist, and the pillars of rock recede into the earth.

Balthasar furrows his brow. "Is this a trick?"

"If we meant you harm, you wouldn't be alive long enough to know it," he replies. "Perhaps you should keep that in mind before your deliver the name to your queen. Perhaps she doesn't deserve it."

Balthasar snorts. "Oh, I know she doesn't deserve it. But she'll only free me if I deliver the right name."

"She has a history of keeping her promises, I take it? Of treating you with respect?"

He averts his eyes, and as he swishes his tongue around in his mouth, tastes the memory of that night in the royal bed—the orgasm built on a broken promise, the hope, the whip. The ogre of loneliness digs into Balthasar's spine as he adjusts his hulking heft, hunching the messenger further.

"You're right," he says to the dwarf. "But I still have a job to do."

Rumpelstiltskin offers a cordial nod and gestures for the boy to continue down the path. The moment he leaps out from beneath the tree, the dwarves disappear and the cave transforms back into a sensible cottage. Balthasar clambers down the hill, racing along the path to the castle, and doesn't stop until he reaches the palace gates. The moon is nearly risen when he collapses at the guards' feet, panting.

"I have it... the name...."

The guards drag Balthasar through the castle to Queen Moira's weaving room and toss him to the floor. His face smacks against the stone, and blood trickles from his nose, but the queen shows no sympathy. Grabbing him by the collar, Moira pulls him to his feet.

"Where have you been, boy? It's nearly time!"

"I'm aware, your majesty."

She shakes him by the shoulders, glaring as she screeches. "Well? What's the name?"

"I'll give it to you," he says. "But I want something first."

"If the name you found works, you can have whatever you want. Leave the kingdom, I don't care. I have no intention of breaking that promise."

"So you've said repeatedly. But just in case you don't, I'm demanding part of my reward now."

He wipes the blood from his nose as he stands, backing the queen against the wall.

"What do you want?" she asks. "I'll do anything to save my son. Name it."

His hand moves down her neck to her breasts. She gasps in shock, but the inhalation becomes more positive when Balthasar's thumb caresses her nipple.

"I've been so lonely," he says. "This stupid mission, all these weeks collecting names for a royal child who isn't even royal, all for you."

Her eyes widen, and Balthasar nods.

"Yes, I know everything, highness, and I think I deserve a little extra for my silence."

When Queen Moira's jaw drops, Balthasar fills her mouth with his eager tongue. She fights it at first, but she soon softens against him.

Their tongues twist together like snakes desperate for warmth, only separating when he presses his hand between her legs.

She throws her head back in ecstasy, and whispers hungrily, "I've been lonely, too. My tryst with the dwarf was the only time I've been happy since my father sold me to the king." Hiking up her skirt, she wraps one leg around Balthasar's waist. "I never wanted this life, messenger. I wanted to explore, to see the wonders of the world. I'm a prisoner here, just like you. And if I lose the baby to the dwarf, the king will surely have me hanged."

"If that's the case, you'd better hold onto whatever pleasure you can."

He unsnaps his braces and lowers his britches. The queen is wet as morning dew when he plunges himself inside her, sighing as the ogre of loneliness melts from his back.

"I've dreamt of this," Balthasar says, thrusting faster. "Through all the days and nights on the road, all this time serving you, and all the promises I knew you'd never keep."

Licking her lips, she whispers, "What do you mean?"

He pulls his cock out of her. Beating it madly, he ejaculates on her gown, and she exhales in confusion.

"You're never going to let me go, are you?" Balthasar asks.

"Of course I will, messenger."

"My name is Balthasar."

Moira presses her lips to his ear and purrs, "Balthasar, I'm yours to command. Just give me the dwarf's name, and I promise I'll let you go."

"You said that last time. And like any man with a queen's come on his face, I believed you. Then you had your bastard guards whip me within an inch of my life."

She lowers her head, nodding sadly. "I'm sorry about that. I just knew how valuable you'd be in the future—"

"Bullshit. You rule me like you rule everyone in this castle." He presses his hand between her thighs again, and she shivers. "But dwarves are immune to your pussy control. You screwed with them, and now you'll pay for your deceptions." Balthasar releases the queen and strides to her loom. Tearing off a piece of gold cloth and tossing it at Moira, Balthasar says, "Clean yourself up before that come's as hard as your heart."

A snicker draws both of their eyes to a shadowy corner, where a stunted man stands.

"Rumpelstiltskin," Balthasar whispers.

"That's his name? Rumpelstiltskin, Rumpelstiltskin!" Queen Moira screams. "Your name is spoken, and our pact is broken!"

The dwarf emerges from the shadows, and Balthasar's brow furrows at the man with the cropped red beard.

"Rumpelstiltskin? You cut your beard."

"What are you talking about? He's always looked like that," the queen snaps.

When Balthasar shakes his head and exhales an apology, Moira whimpers.

"It's not the right name, is it?"

"No, it isn't, your majesty," the dwarf replies proudly.

"But Rumpelstiltskin sang of spinning straw to gold. He mentioned stealing a child."

"Both are common practices among our people, my dear boy," the dwarf says. Glancing out the window at the peaking moon, he sighs through a smile. "That should do it."

"My baby—"

"No, *my* baby," he says. "And he's gone, my love, but you needn't fear for his safety. We shall raise him up into a fine dwarven man, and one day, he'll be able to trick humans with the best of them."

"No, I won't let you!"

She dives at the dwarf, but when he lifts his hands, chunks of rock dislodge from the wall and launch at the queen's head. They smack her to the floor, where she cries in pain. Balthasar doesn't exactly feel bad for her, but when she snivels more for her baby than her leaking skull, his heart aches.

"Halencia," he says, and the dwarf's ears perk. "She escaped your curse by agreeing to become a dwarf companion, right?"

"Yes. And?"

"Surely you have room for another. Then the queen could live near her child."

Moira lifts her head in hope as the dwarf strokes his blunted beard.

"I suppose we could take on another lover. Halencia does get tired something awful."

The queen scrunches herself up on her knees, her hands clasped in prayer.

"Please, take me to my son. I'll do whatever you wish."

The dwarf strides over and caresses beneath her chin. "Yes, you will, my darling. And you'll love every second of it." Glinting an incisor, he nods at Balthasar. "As for you, what can I give in exchange for your silence on this incident?"

Balthasar smiles, and the dwarf nods knowingly.

"Consider freedom yours, at long last, young man."

He winks as he kisses Moira, and in a flash of golden light, the dwarf and the queen disappear. A furious rapping on the door rattles Balthasar's bones, and his heart races when he hears someone boom, "In the name of the king, open this door!"

Inspecting the room, he sees no escape, and as the knocks become stronger it appears the door might smash inward. But a blast of light fills the room again. It surrounds Balthasar, and his skin tingles as his solidity fades. He doesn't have time to be afraid before his vision cuts out, but he doubts he would fear it anyway—for within the bizarre magic, there are gusts of unfamiliar air. The unfamiliar is new, and all things new trumpet freedom.

When Balthasar feels the ground beneath him again, he finds himself standing on the edge of a forest, with the castle of Auralom a miniscule spot of white in the distance. His heart thumps madly against his chest, and he leaps into the air, hooting and hollering in joy. He's still alone, but the sign declaring, "Two Miles to Zadaroze" ahead warms him more than any woman he's known.

He parades to town, his head held high. A few of the small shops scattered through the forest along the main drag in Zadaroze sport signs seeking employment, but a storefront with the mirrored "help wanted" sign plucks Balthasar's interest most. Staring through the window, he tries to discern the manner of merchandise, until someone taps his shoulder.

Balthasar turns to behold a voluptuous brunette with doe eyes who coos, "May I help you, sir?"

Focusing on her glistening lips and buxom charms, he loses his words for a moment. He gathers his wits and clears his throat. "What do you sell here, miss?"

"Magic mirrors mostly, and other enchanted objects," she replies.

"And you have an opening to fill?"

She giggles as she dances her fingers across her collarbone. "I do indeed." Taking Balthasar's hand, she says, "Come inside, sir, and show me what you can do."

"I'm afraid I don't have much experience."

"Lucky for you I'm a good teacher," she says and pulls him through the door. "Plus, we can use all the help we can get today. The king of Zadaroze has just commissioned a mirror for his daughter, Snow White."

Of Greed and Eager Things

by Edda Grenade

FOR THREE DAYS, BENHADAD had fled his responsibilities. On the eve of the third night, a pack of jackals found him.

They were not the small, pale-brown things that sometimes intruded into the outer districts of his home city, Bab-Ilim, and ravaged the chickens. These were black-backed, great-jawed jackals, their shoulders of a height with his.

Benhadad's stomach turned with fear as they circled him and his ibex, their tongues lolling. Panting. They smelled of sweat and musk and rotten flesh, and they looked *very* hungry.

The river along which he had been riding the past days was right there, but its bank was a cliff, here, and Benhadad was not certain he would be able to swim with all his clothes and weapons and his pack, he had never properly learned how—

There was another sound, besides the jackals' rasping wet breaths. Hooves, galloping. An arrow whistled past Benhadad and embedded itself into a beast's flank. It yowled and leaped to the side, startling the others into frenzy.

When a second arrow hit the ground where another jackal had stood half a moment before, Benhadad threw himself flat to the earth. His heart hammered in his chest, but it seemed like....

Another arrow, into flesh. The jackals yowled and fled. Too late Benhadad realized that his ibex, too, had taken flight. He heaved himself to his feet again, yelling hoarsely after the steed, but it was in vain. It was already too far gone in its fear.

His shoulder sagging in defeat, he turned to see who had saved him—and pulled himself to his full height when he saw the two great antelopes that were trotting towards him. One of them carried two thick saddlebags, the other a smaller set of saddlebags and a rider who was holding a short bow across their lap.

The rider's arms were bare, and Benhadad saw that their skin was far darker than even his own, like black garnet. It was an elven woman, he realized as they came closer, and a *roamer* of all things. She bore no sign of any tribe, only a dusty cloak over a riding dress and trousers that looked like they had seen better days.

Even with his legs and back straight, his head barely reached to the antelopes' shoulders. Benhadad made an effort to appear as dignified as possible despite his heart still rattling in his ribcage. He was painfully aware of how dirtied his clothes were, hopelessly smudged with mud at the knees from drinking from the river like a peasant. Even if he wished to be as far removed as possible from the royal heritage that awaited him back in Bab-Ilim for the moment, there was no need to let a roamer see him in such a miserable state.

The antelope that bore only saddlebags sidled up close to him until the elf called it back. The language was not one Benhadad knew, but it sounded similar to the one the elven ambassadors who came for trade to Bab-Ilim used. The elf dismounted when she reached him, casting her gaze wide over the plains into the direction in which the jackals had fled.

She turned to him, deftly loosing the string of her bow as she walked, and spoke to him, again in that elvish language.

"I apologize," Benhadad said, "I don't speak your language, but I—"

"Are you all right?"

Surprised, Benhadad stopped mid-sentence. He had not expected her to know the eastern traders' tongue, or for her voice to curl so smoothly around the words.

"Yes," he replied in the same language and bowed slightly. "I thank you for your help."

She shrugged. "I was hunting them anyway. 'Tis a bit of a pity they ran, though, now I'll have to run them down again...."

"You were... hunting them?"

"Yes, their pelts sell for a pretty coin in the mountains west of here." She was wrapping the string along her bow, eyes cast down on the work. "I'm Sekhet. What's your name?"

"Benhadad," he replied, and nearly had to bite his tongue so he would not add, 'Prince of the Elder House of Bab-Ilim,' out of years-long habit.

"And what are you doing all alone by the Grey River, Benhadad? The jackals are plenty, these months."

"I was... traveling. I have family in Bab-Ilim."

"Ah." The elf did not call him foolish for carrying such a paltry quantity of provisions with him, which he had half expected. She did look him up and down with a thoughtful expression, but he could detect no flicker of recognition in her eyes as they passed over the bracelet on his wrist that marked him as a member of dwarven royalty.

"You won't get much farther in the light today, and it's a few days yet to Bab-Ilim. You can share my camp tonight, if you wish," she offered.

Benhadad's skin felt like it was stretched a little too tight over his bones, his heartbeat still thudding quickly. A roamer would likely not feel beholden to the laws of hospitality; they had no reason to fear the wrath of jinns or the sanctions of allies and trading partners if they harmed those whom they had offered shelter and food, for roamers called nothing their house.

But then, the elf *had* saved him....

"Thank you," he said quietly. "I shall."

THEY TRAVELED NORTH along the river for a little while, the same path Benhadad had taken only a few hours before, but night was falling fast, and soon the elf decided she would make camp close to the cliff of the riverside. A small path carved its way into a crevice of the cliff there, leading down to the water at a gentle slope. She unstrapped the saddlebags and saddle from the antelopes, placed them on the ground, and shooed the animals to drink.

The place was not protected by any natural structures, but then again, few places were in the great plain of the Grey River. Benhadad's ibex would have been able to scale the cliffside regardless of the presence of a track, since it was bred for the steep and winding paths in the mountains that surrounded Bab-Ilim, but the elf's antelopes were not so dexterous.

Benhadad watched as the elf spread out her bedroll, feeling superfluous. Then she retrieved an intricately decorated lantern from her packs and set it on the ground before the bedroll. Intrigued, he stepped closer.

"Is that jinn's fire?"

The elf nodded as she opened the lantern and lit the sparkwool inside. "I don't usually need the light, but it keeps jackals away and you need the warmth."

"I don't—"

"You're shivering. It's the fear, it leaves slowly sometimes."

Benhadad swallowed his reply. He was shivering, a little, so he seated himself close to the fire once it flared. He pulled his cloak underneath him, rubbing his arms. Rare and expensive, the jinn's fire made him wonder how she had come by it, and why—

"Why don't you need the light?"

"Because I don't," she said with a grin, leaning over him to stir the sparkwool. The fire was still small, and in the amber darkness of twilight her eyes were almost entirely pupil, with only a thin ring of golden iris visible. She smelled of wood smoke, the dust of the plains, blade oil, and pack animal, and underneath it all was the faint curl of old blood.

Benhadad could feel himself blush, and he surreptitiously tried to lean away. Sekhet did not seem to be embarrassed by their closeness, nor by the fact that he had practically *scented* her.

"You look like you've never seen one of my kind before," she commented.

"I haven't... not very many."

Not this close.

"I haven't encountered too many dwarrows, either." Sekhet dug a parcel of dried fish and nuts from her saddlebags, then took a seat on her bedroll on the other side of the fire and continued, "Most of the stories about your people are spun from either very pretty or very ugly yarn, depending on who tells them. But it's likely the same with elves."

Benhadad looked down at his lap. "It's not... I don't fear you for that. It's just that there are no pretty stories about roamers."

She chuckled and held up a piece of dried fish. "Why don't you tell me some of those stories, for a bit of fish?"

There were still sticks of honey-cured meat in Benhadad's own small pack, but he suspected this was not about food, not really. Sekhet seemed genuinely curious. He accepted the deal, and over the course of the next hour he told her as many tales of the dangers and wickedness of roamers as he could remember while they shared the dried fish between them. He almost managed to forget why he was out here in the first place—why he had fled his home and family. But as distracting as Sekhet's attention was, it could not erase the memory of those seven awful days when Benhadad had been forced to assume that he was next in line for the throne.

He was the queen's third child, and he had never expected nor wanted the crown. His grandmother had ruled for long, long years before his mother had ever taken the throne, but then his father had passed from sickness, his eldest sister had forsaken her beard and claim to the throne for the right to practice the sacred magic of the Jinnirei... and then, ten days ago, the missive came that the queen and her second-eldest daughter had been attacked while traveling in the northern mountains.

After a week of uncertainty, Benhadad had been sick with fear. Even the news that his mother and sister were alive could not soothe him... and so he ran.

He could not reveal any of this to Sekhet, who knew what a roamer might think to do when she realized she had a prince in her company, but the way she treated him—with no special care, like an equal—lightened his chest immensely.

While he talked, she laughed, sometimes, the sound sharp and ragged and the smile that accompanied it unexpectedly wide. Benhadad found that he liked seeing it.

When the fish and nuts were gone and the antelopes had made their way back up from the river and laid themselves down next to the saddlebags, a gentle silence grew between them. Until Sekhet spoke again, in a fashion that sounded deliberately casual.

"I've heard some stories about your people," she said. "Stories about how you're made of stone between the legs. I was wondering if they were true."

Something squirmed deep in Benhadad's belly. Sekhet met his eyes without hesitation, and her gaze was intense in a way he had not seen before. She leaned back to brace herself on her hands, legs sprawled lazily before her. There was no self-consciousness in her face, but there was something else....

It was greed, and not for riches.

"We're not," he said, his voice gone thin. His cheeks felt very warm. "It's all flesh and blood like the rest of us."

"Is it indeed," murmured Sekhet, and Benhadad's chest grew tight with the stirrings of arousal as she continued to watch him. He had no memory of ever having such open desire directed at him.

She doesn't know, he thought. *Of course she would be bold, I'm just an unlucky traveler to her.* Sekhet did not know the meaning of his bracelet, nor of the crown that might one day circle his head. She did not know of the helpless, selfish fear that had taken root in Benhadad's belly when he had realized how close he was to being made king. She would never see him again, once they parted ways.

He was no prince to her, which was as good as not being a prince at all, now. A prince would feel no urge to dally with a roamer, and even less an urge to be caught underneath said roamer.

Benhadad looked at the strange length of Sekhet's body, at her smile, and at the corded muscle in her arms, and thought that he very much wanted to be caught.

"Would—would you like proof?" he asked, hating how unsteady and young he sounded. Sekhet's smile skewed into a smirk.

"I'd like to bed you," she said quietly.

A soft breath shuddered out of Benhadad as his cock grew warm and heavy between his legs.

"I'd like that," he managed.

"Come here, then." She sat up again and he hastened around the fire and dropped to his knees at her side. Though she sat upon her buttocks while he knelt, she was still taller than him. Having to look up at her sent a small thrill of excitement down Benhadad's spine. He was not used to partners who were larger than him, but the few times it had happened in the past... he had reveled in it.

Sekhet placed one of her hands lightly on the side of his neck, leaned towards him.

"How do dwarrows hold with kissing?"

"I hold it in high regard," replied Benhadad, his chin hitching up in anticipation.

When Sekhet finally cupped his face in her hands and bent to kiss him, he nearly whimpered. Then she stroked one hand through his beard and down his neck, his chest and belly, down between his legs, and he did whimper into the kiss. They broke apart and she rested her forehead against his so they were sharing air.

This close, he could smell her arousal easily. It was not so different from a dwarrowdam's scent, salty and half made of sweat, but to his surprise it was thicker, headier, and the air between them was heavy with it. The scent, her closeness, and the knowledge of how fiercely she desired him made Benhadad's cock fat with blood, and he ached for a touch.

"Tell me, what do you want?" she asked him.

"A-anything you'd have of me...."

"That's a dangerously generous offer, Benhadad," she whispered against his lips; her voice was rough and low.

"What *would* you have of me, then?"

She squeezed him lightly—her hand was not as broad as a dwarrow's but her fingers were long and just as powerful—and he grasped eagerly at her shoulders, another noise tumbling from his mouth.

"I don't have much interest in being breached, even if you weren't so thick all over," she murmured. Benhadad pulled back in confusion.

"Why would you want to lie with me if I'm too thick?"

"I love how thick you are, and how well this prick of yours fits my hand," she said with another squeeze of his cock while her other arm snaked about his back to pull him close against her body. She leaned over him and slowly tipped him over onto his back. Benhadad held tight to her shoulders.

"I love how strong and sturdy you are, and yet how *small*...." Then her weight settled on top of his body, pressed him down half into the dry grass, half into the bedroll, and Benhadad arched up for another kiss that Sekhet gave him easily. She kissed him so deeply it made his head swim, tongue twining against the roof of his mouth.

"I just don't like a fat prick inside of me," she said when she pulled back, "I'd much rather fuck you." Benhadad felt himself flush from his hairline to his nipples, and his cock twitched where it was trapped between their bellies.

"You—you wish to take me?"

"Yes. Is that—"

"Gods, *yes*," he breathed, and Sekhet laughed in delight while her scent thickened yet further. She kissed him again, a short press of lips that were stretched in a smile, and then she rose to her feet. Benhadad watched with his heart fluttering in his chest as she bent over one of the saddlebags. The antelopes still lounged right beside them. One of them had laid its head upon the lower flank of its companion and appeared to be dozing, while the other chewed lazily. They did not look like they minded that their owner was having a tumble in front of them. Benhadad, on the other hand, felt his cheeks heat again; animals though they were, he could not help but be self-conscious at the thought of rutting in front of them.

When Sekhet had finished rummaging in her saddlebag and returned, however, she rubbed her palm over the wakeful antelope's snout in passing. She did not seem to mind their presence, and that eased Benhadad's embarrassment.

She deposited a metal tin and a bag of silvery cloth next to the bedroll before kneeling down and pulling Benhadad to straddle her thighs. She held him with both hands, her fingers spread wide over his buttocks. Even through two layers of fabric he could feel her heat, and the last traces of his embarrassment fled. She nuzzled the crook of his neck where his skin was not hidden by beard or hair or cloth and informed him that he was free to undress himself.

"I've no fondness for fiddling with that much knotwork," she added, and Benhadad had to grin.

"There's a trick to opening it," he said. He opened his belt, freed one string from the bottom of his vest, undid the topmost knot, and tugged at the string: one by one, the knots came loose and his vest gaped open. Sekhet made a small sound of appreciation as he shed it. Next came his overshirt and long tunic, and then he was naked from the waist up. The night air was cool, but not enough to hesitate over disrobing.

Sekhet leaned back, her gaze wandering over his bare skin—then it caught on his nipples, where two small silver studs gleamed amidst the dark hairs of his chest.

"You can touch them," Benhadad said softly and shivered as she reached up and tugged at the left one, gently, then harder when he moaned out a small *"Yes."* The sweet sting of it only became sweeter with every repeat. Eventually Sekhet hauled him close again and put her mouth—and *teeth*—where her fingers had been. Benhadad groaned, clutching at her shoulders.

"I want to—ah—touch you as well," he managed, tugging at the fabric of her clothes. Sekhet let him go and together they lifted her dress over her head. The rest of their clothes followed quickly, piled in a heap beside the bedroll, and then he was naked on his back and she was above him, her body blotting out the stars. She was so *tall*.

"Come, touch me," Sekhet whispered.

There was so much skin that Benhadad did not quite know where to start. After a moment's awkward pause he placed one palm on the side of her neck, like she had done in the beginning. Soon he discovered that she enjoyed being stroked, so he spent time running his hands over every inch of her skin he could reach while she nuzzled and nipped at his throat. It was almost languid, the way the moved against one another, and Benhadad's arousal simmered low but hot, his shaft half-hard against his thigh.

He found that Sekhet's body lacked proper hair, too. Only between her legs and under her arms could he find little patches of dark, curly hair. Her muscles were sinewy where he was used to bulk, her limbs long and thin instead of short and stout, her entire form so alien to him... and yet Benhadad wanted her inside him very much indeed.

When she rolled onto her back, pulling him with her, his thigh dragged against her sex, his cock across her stomach, and Benhadad was not the only one to make a noise at the friction. She was sopping wet, and when she asked to open him up, Benhadad very nearly begged.

Sekhet reached for the metal tin, popping off its lid. The distinct smell of blade oil filled the air and Benhadad's cock gave a helpless twitch where it lay against her hip, fully hard once more.

"How long has it been?" she asked him as she spread him open, greased fingers prodding at his hole. He arched into the touch.

"Almost—almost a year since I've had anything larger than two fingers."

"Do you need me to be careful?"

"I need you to *hurry*. Please, I want you inside me...."

Benhadad had not thought it possible for Sekhet's pupils to grow even larger, but they did. The utter hunger with which she looked at him then left his belly shivering.

The first finger stung from his body's disuse and tense anticipation, but even with the awkward angle she found the spot where he was the most sensitive and rubbed the top of a fingernail across it. The second finger went in easy, although all too soon Sekhet muttered something that sounded suspiciously like a curse and withdrew from him.

"My fingers will cramp if I continue like this," she explained before he had a chance to ask. "Get on your belly, and I'll get you nice and open...." Benhadad let out a sound that was half-groan half-chuckle and climbed from her lap to lie on the bedroll. His hips tilted up almost of their own volition.

"Like a cat in heat," Sekhet murmured, smiling, and rather than be insulted Benhadad raised his hips higher. She shifted until she lay on her side next to him and slipped three fingers back inside him, while her second hand squirmed beneath his chest to play with the metal studs in his nipples. He moaned and shuddered as she curled her fingers down, this time digging them into his sweet spot.

"I'm going to fuck you like this," she told him quietly, "with you on your belly, arching up so I can get at your little baubles."

"Yes, yes—oh—" He whimpered when suddenly four fingers were spreading him, and the thought of being pinned beneath her, of getting pinned by her cock had Benhadad's own leaking messily onto the bedroll.

"I'm ready, I'm ready—"

Sekhet made an eager little noise and pushed her fingertips down one last time before she withdrew. He was wet, slick with oil and stretched open so that her departing hand left him feeling utterly empty. He squirmed in place as Sekhet sat up and reached for the cloth bag. She fiddled with it, drawing it open and spreading it out into a square, its contents bared.

"Come and pick one," she called.

In the bag was a mess of interconnected leather straps, something like a harness he had seen before, and next to it lay three cocks of different shapes, all as dark as Sekhet's skin.

She stroked an oily hand down his spine, fingers teasing against the rim of his hole as she pressed a soft kiss to his temple.

"Which one do you want?"

"I...." The first one was long and slim, with a gentle upwards curve. The second was a little shorter and thicker, though still thinner than Benhadad's own, and sloped downwards. The last one was short, especially compared to the great length of Sekhet's body, and fat, with a pronounced head. A soft, high exhale went from Benhadad's throat.

"This one," he whispered and picked up the shortest.

Sekhet took it from him with a wink. The business of fitting it into the leather harness and fitting the harness about her hips took long enough that Benhadad pressed close to her in his eagerness, kissing her and thoroughly getting in the way. "Just like a cat," she remarked, but the noise she made when he dragged his lips into the crook of her neck was like gravel.

Once it was done, he dipped his fingers in the tin of blade oil. When he wrapped his slick palm around the toy her hips jerked forward and she groaned, head dropping. Benhadad went very still and looked up at her face, staring at her closed eyes and open mouth.

"Can you," he almost stuttered, "you can feel that?"

"Yes," sighed Sekhet, and her hips hitched forward again, sliding the shaft through Benhadad's slack grip.

"How?"

"It's... I don't know the proper word for it in this language, but it's *mine*. It belongs to my blood," she said, her eyes blinking open to look at him. "It was a gift from a lover, quite the skilled woodcarver she was, and it's *mine*...."

His throat went dry and he squeezed his hands around Sekhet's cock until she let out another noise. The object was made of lacquered wood and thus far less yielding and not as warm as something of flesh and blood might have been, but it had been carved with an astonishing attention to detail—he traced veins on the underside, folds of skin below the head, the slit at the tip. It occurred to Benhadad that she might well be larger *everywhere* than anyone else he had ever taken before, and the thought made him ache with need.

Yet still he lingered on the task of slicking her with oil for longer than necessary, entranced by the sounds this pulled from her and the way her face went slack with pleasure when he rubbed the pad of his thumb back and forth over the tip of her cock.

"Don't tease," she eventually ground out, though she did not appear to be very upset. Benhadad found himself smiling, half in sheepishness, half in wanton hunger.

"Will you take me now?" he breathed.

"As soon as you get on your belly." She did not have to tell him twice, and he drew his legs together on one side of her, only to have her grab him by the waist and flip him the rest of the way with an ease that startled and exited him at once. He came to rest in the same spot on the bedroll where he had lain when she had fingered him open. Under his belly the cloth was still wet from before.

Sekhet braced herself on the small of his back with a hand as she swung one leg across his to straddle his thighs, pinning him with her weight. Benhadad whined and arched, but then the weight was gone and he could feel her breath upon his ear.

"Are you all right?" she asked quietly.

"Yes, I—I'm—" He was stammering, gone breathless with lust, and it took him a moment to form proper words: "You may—you can—please put your hand back there." Sekhet was still for a moment, until she did as he asked; placed her hand squarely in the small of his back and rested her weight on it, her cock nudging against the backs of his thighs. The way she pressed down on him forced his own hard cock tight against the bedroll, almost heavy enough to be uncomfortable, but like this... he was truly caught.

"Like this? As though I'm holding you down?"

Benhadad moaned helplessly. "Yes, gods, take me now."

"We shall see," she said, a laugh in her voice. "You teased me quite a lot before, perhaps I should have turnabout."

"W-what?"

Sekhet's hips curled back and forth as she ground her cock between his buttocks, the wet tip catching on the rim of his hole again and again but never breaching. Her mouth dragged hot and wet along the shell of his ear. "I could fuck between your thighs until I've taken my pleasure like that, and leave you to rut into the bedroll like a fledgling."

Benhadad whined in frustration as her cock once again slid past its mark.

"Please Sekhet, *please* take me," he begged. She shivered above him, stilling.

"Show me where you want me."

"Inside, *inside*...."

"Show me," she whispered, in a voice gone ragged like crushed rock.

With effort, Benhadad fumbled his hands back and behind him. His fingers dug into the meat of his buttocks, pulling them apart to show Sekhet where he was wet and open and so, so greedy to be filled. His body arched with the movement, legs spreading as far as they could between Sekhet's thighs and his breath coming noisily. Part of him—the part that was *prince* before it was *Benhadad*—writhed in shame at how wanton and desperate to be subdued he was. It screamed at him that no prince of such old blood as his should act this way. But the rest of him was ready and willing to beg Sekhet again.

He got his wish as she nudged the fat head of her cock into his hole. Benhadad could only gasp for air—she was big, and it burned as it went in, but once the head slipped wholly past the ring of muscle the pleasure of finally being taken overwhelmed all else. The royal voice drowned in the throb of his blood.

He went loose under her, hands falling to grasp weakly at the bedroll. Slowly, gently, she rocked deeper into him until Benhadad keened when the tip of her cock nudged over his sweet spot.

"Benhadad," Sekhet breathed, "Benhadad, Benhadad," and then the skin of her hips met his buttocks and Benhadad nearly wailed with how filled he was. More than he had ever been before, he was sure. His skin felt like stars were trapped beneath it, prickling and overheated.

For a few long, torturous moments she remained motionless, and then she pushed her free hand under his chest to twist one pierced nipple.

"Ah, Se—Sekhet," he grit out through clenched teeth. He was so desperate for her to move, even though he knew that he would embarrass himself by screaming as soon as she did.

"Don't worry about the noise," she whispered. "The fire will keep the jackals away, even if you howl...."

"Sekhet," he moaned, like her name was a plea all on its own.

Suddenly the sweat-slick heat of her body was all along his back and she was moving, the angle of her hips shifting so that her cock bore straight down inside him, right where it made him keen. And keen he did, loud and shameless and as though he was wounded. He was trapped between her body and the ground, her breasts pressed to the back of his shoulders by the arm she had slung around his ribcage. Her heartbeat fluttered against his spine and she panted, stilling again, her jaw resting against his temple.

"Move," he begged in every language he knew, "*Move*, I won't break—"

Sekhet did. Hips rising, she let her cock drag from his body until the head stretched him wide again. Then, hips sinking, she pierced him again. Benhadad's cock leaked, drooling into the bedroll and staining his stomach wet. He clutched at her hand where it splayed against his chest, and at the back of her neck, frantic for something to hold on to.

She was whispering to him in between harsh breaths and softer sighs. He heard his name in amongst words he did not understand, but the way she spoke set him alight. She sweated onto his skin, the thick, dizzying scent of her desire enfolding them so that he knew he would carry it for days. The thought made him clench and arch, and Sekhet shuddered on top of him. He wanted to feel this for days to come.

"*Harder*," he gasped, "harder, harder...!"

The strength of Sekhet's thrusts grew with every plea, though when she withdrew it was still with a nigh paradoxical gentleness, like the inhale before a scream. A slow drag out, a harsh thrust in.

Every stab of her cock forced a cry from him and pleasure into his body. He felt as though he was fraying apart at the seams, every thrust too much and yet every time Sekhet hilted herself he thought he could never have enough of it. He kept begging, though he could not be sure of what tongue the words were that fell from his mouth.

When he came it was thunderous and without warning, like a cave-in. He sobbed as Sekhet rutted him through it, his body wracked with shudders, the breath too thin in his lungs.

Once the shudders waned he collapsed, too wrecked to even hold on to her. His entire body was ablaze with the blissful ache of fading orgasm and Sekhet was warm and heavy and taut with tension above him.

"Wait," he rasped when she moved to withdraw from him. "Wait, there's no need!"

"I'd rather not—not hurt you in my hunger," she said, though she stilled with the crown of her shaft still just inside him. Her hips were trembling. Benhadad turned his head so he could look up at her, taking in her blown-wide pupils, panting mouth, and the thin sheen of sweat that covered her skin. With great effort he managed to reach back with one hand, laying it on her hip to tug her in again.

"I would have you take your pleasure."

Sekhet relaxed incrementally and Benhadad mewled as she pressed fully into him again. There was a smile lurking in the corners of her mouth now.

"You're a greedy thing, aren't you," she murmured.

Yes, Benhadad thought as he canted his hips up best as he could under her weight so she slipped even deeper. *Yes, I am.* She made a low noise, fumbling for a grip on his waist—and when she found it, she gave him all.

These were not the long, deep hard strokes of earlier but quick short jabs. They drove the air from his lungs in whimpers. He was sensitive and exhausted, the thrusts making him ache and burn, but his blood sang with his willingness to take it. To his delight Sekhet's breathing soon grew jagged, her rhythm frantic. When she let out a low, rumbling moan that shook her body Benhadad bit his lips on a gasp, insides clenching around her. He imagined he could almost feel her spending inside him, her fluids pushed deeper with ever-gentling thrusts.

For long minutes they lay under the stars while their breath and strength returned. When she eventually pulled out of him it made a filthy wet sound and pulled a harsh whimper from his lips. Benhadad let himself lay there a moment longer, enjoying the tender, used feeling of his hole before he rolled onto his back and sat up.

Sekhet critically eyed the soiled spot on the bedroll and then sighed. With an absent hand she stroked under Benhadad's jaw, fingers carding through his beard before she bent to kiss him.

"Come, we'll have to clean this, and ourselves," she said, and laughed when Benhadad cupped her face to keep her there for another kiss.

"In a moment," he mumbled, smiling against her mouth. "I don't think I can stand yet. Or walk, for that matter, you were so rough." It was only half a joke; his legs felt quite shaky, and he sat on the side of one thigh so no pressure was put upon his buttocks.

"Was I too—"

"No, gods no." Quietly, he added: "I love how rough you were. And how tall and strong you are...."

Sekhet said nothing for a moment, only looked at him with her dark, dark eyes.

"I suppose," she began, "I suppose I'll have to carry you down to the water?"

"That will likely be necessary, yes," he replied, laughing.

"And tomorrow... how will you make for Bab-Ilim if you cannot walk properly? The city is far, yet."

Benhadad went warm all over. Almost he wondered if his bracelet would burn his wrist for the indignity he had visited upon the royal body, but here... here he was no prince, nor would be again till he stepped through the gates of Bab-Ilim.

He did not tell her that he would be able to walk easily with little pain on the morrow—let her think him less hardy than the truth. Being thought delicate gave him a special thrill and he smiled.

"If... if you were to accompany me, I could reach it easily within a few days," he murmured. "And my family is—is not poor, I'm sure I could compensate you for the loss of the jackal furs."

"Are you sure you want a lawless roamer as your traveling companion?" Sekhet asked, but now she was grinning too. Benhadad's mouth stretched wider to match hers and he slung his arms about her shoulders, lacing his fingers together behind her neck.

"I want *you* as my traveling companion."

I want you to lie with me again, he did not say, but from the way she kissed him then he suspected she knew.

Contributors

Jason Carpenter is an award-winning journalist who grew up on a steady diet of romance novels and trashy soaps. He traded in his press badge for a hotel room key and he now writes, as well as lives, erotic adventures.

Julie Cox, author of "Wizard's Staff," has a number of fantasy, sci-fi, and/or erotic works published with Circlet Press and elsewhere. Her work can be found at writingwhilehuman.com, and she is on Twitter as @SQLPi. Her novel, *Capricious*, won the 2014 Best Bisexual Book Award for erotica and is also available in audio via nobilis.libsyn.com. She is an activist for progressive ideals and lives in Texas with her children and many pets.

Edda Grenade is person of mystery.

Lacey P. Jeffers is the fun and more adventurous alter ego of Eva Eldridge, who works as a telcom engineer during the day. When she isn't busy paying the bills, she travel writes for BigBlendMagazines.com. Eva has had stories and poems published in SandScript, a college arts and literary magazine. She continues to take classes at the local community college and has embarked on editing other people's writing. Southern Arizona called to Eva in the late 1970s, and she continues to live there with her husband and animals. Her website is evaeldridge.com[1], her blog is evaeldridgethreesidesto.com[2], and her Twitter is @ThreeSidesTo.

Bess Lyre is an Australian author with a weakness for Norse mythology. She has squeezed herself down the narrowest street in

---

1. http://evaeldridge.com/

2. http://evaeldridgethreesidesto.com/

Gamla Stan, Stockholm, fed reindeer in Northern Lapland, and partied under the midnight sun in Tromsø, Norway. "Ash and Elm" is her first published erotic story.

Alanna McFall is an actor and writer based out of the Bay Area in California. She has published pieces in *Mad Scientist Journal, Escape Pod, Alliteration Ink,* and many more. You can follow her work on her website at https://alannamcfall.wordpress.com[3] or on Twitter at @AlannaMcFall.

Jessica McHugh is an author of speculative fiction spanning genres from horror and alternate history to epic fantasy. A prolific writer, she has devoted herself to novels, short stories, poetry, and playwriting. She has had sixteen books published in six years, including the *Rabbits in the Garden,* her bizarro sci-fi novel *The Green Kangaroos,* and the first book in her edgy YA series, *Darla Decker Diaries.* Learn more at http://www.jessicamchughbooks.com/

TS Porter is a tiny geek frequently mistaken for a collection of knobbly twigs wearing glasses. When not sleeping, they are usually found obsessively writing or baking sweet delicacies. TS's physical location and momentum varies, but home is always online. They can be found at ts-porter.tumblr.com[4].

3.   https://alannamcfall.wordpress.com/

4.   http://ts-porter.tumblr.com/

Other Circlet Books You May Enjoy

What Happens at the Tavern, Stays at the Tavern $5.99

Since Tolkien's time, many authors have taken readers along on elaborate treks through fantastic worlds. In "What Happens at the Tavern Stays at the Tavern," we asked writers to tackle the pauses and interstices in a fantasy quest. What kinds of steamy adventures happen behind the scenes, when our heroes and heroines are trekking along their journey?

Like a Sword $4.99

Sword & Sorcery stories that swirl with sensuality. These are tales of mages and magic, of warriors and princes and forest folk. But not all battles are won with armies, and magic finds its power not just in heart and soul but in body and desire. Four erotic short stories from some well-known erotica writers and some newcomers: Jason Rubis, Jean Roberta, Argus Marks, and ADR Forte.

Like a Queen $5.99

Five lesbian fairytales that feature classic stories like "Cinderella" and "The Princess and the Pea" with a queer twist. What are the erotic possibilities of the enchanted princesses and forbidding queens that we learned about as children? Discover the love story between Gretel and the Witch and the intoxicating tale of Cinderella's seductively severe stepmother. It wasn't a pea in her mattress that kept the Princess up all night, and the story didn't end when the Prince found Snow White in the woods. Instead of competing for princes or beauty, the women in these stories are made more powerful by their desire for each other.

Like a Prince $5.99

Five gay fairy tales that feature classic stories like "The Beauty and the Beast" and "Cinderella" with a queer twist. What are the erotic possibilities of the dashing princes and dark forbidden forests that we learned about as children? Stories range from the charming tale of a mischievous Cinderella to the deliciously dark story of a modern-day Little Red Riding Hood complete with a real-life wolf. A mysterious young prince needs help from a beautiful young king in "The Goose Boy," and Beauty and the Beast gets a sexy retelling in "Captivated." Includes stories by Elizabeth Schechter, Julie Cox, Kiernan Kelly, Alexandra Erin, and Monique Poirier.

About the Publisher

Circlet Press: Erotica for Geeks. All genres, all genders. Circlet Press has been publishing fine quality erotic science fiction, fantasy, and genre literature since 1992. We love a good sexy story, well told, that sparks the imagination.

www.ingramcontent.com/pod-product-compliance
Lightning Source LLC
Chambersburg PA
CBHW070752180626
46818CB00007B/3084